FUTURE SKINNY

PETER ROSCH

FUTURE SKINNY

Copyright © 2022 by Peter Rosch

All rights reserved.

This is a work of fiction. Names, characters, businesses, organizations, places, events, and incidents either are the product of the author's imagination or are used fictitiously. Any resemblance to actual persons, living or dead, events, or locales is entirely coincidental.

Cover Art by Matthew Revert

Published by Art Cult Books, Wimberley, TX

ISBN: 979-8-9854739-0-2

First edition: May 2022

Published in the United States of America

Library of Congress Control Number: 2022903243

For anyone who knows mirrors are filthy liars.

FUTURE SKINNY

Man starts over again everyday, in spite of all he knows, against all he knows.

—Emil Cioran

1

There he is.

The hotel room is dim, but Casey isn't hard to find.

His body is a beacon of desperate protest underneath a forgiving silk tee. Bone thin. Skin bagging from every corner of his six-foot frame. A good guess would be one-hundred and twenty pounds. He has more hair, just not on his head. Fuzzy wisps of keratin on his arms and thick on the nape of his neck. Inky around the eyes, a dire pigmentation that frames the focus he is straining to hold on the stranger at the other end of the makeshift dining table.

Casey is binge-reading still, and by the look of him, he has been binge-reading far too often.

The spread between the two men is huge, was huge, most of the food has already been eaten.

The client's eyes are wide but unmoved by the brittle hands Casey is using in lieu of utensils. The fingers clutching each next bite are topped with nail beds of blue. The knuckles on his index and middle are callused to the point of deformity. This client's indifference is nothing new. Like all customers, he is there to hear his future. It has never mattered how the pig is slaughtered so long as the bacon tastes good.

Lylian is there too. She hasn't left Casey yet, though their age difference looks as if it's somehow doubled. Longer hair now, green eyes still bright, the only authentic shines in the room. Her arms are firmly folded atop a roadblock stance halfway between the client and the front door. At her size, her posture is hardly intimidating, but for someone so small, she can explode big.

The air stinks. It isn't just the food. Beyond cooling grease and the chemically crafted scents of take-out littered about the table, the odors turn human quick. Inhale like you mean it and you can smell the sin. A half-century's worth of intimacy baking in the manufactured heat of the room's lone window unit.

The repugnant bouquet is married to the chomp, smack, and slurp of Casey's consumption. He is eating hard. He is swallowing fast. Wet. In fact, everything feels wet. Rooms like this one have a squish to them that is everlasting. Stray spit won't make much difference.

The bathroom door behind Casey is open. For now, the smell of upchuck is faint, maybe imagined. There is a beige sink, a matching toilet, and a poky little tub with a basin too small for anyone un-elfin. Any of the three are good for vomit. If Casey were to make sick prematurely, the carpet underfoot would hide it well: it's a synthetic jumble of colors expertly designed to disappear manmade soils. Casey has a twenty-three-gallon Rubbermaid imitation at his side, just in case. Its corner-store price tag hasn't been removed. Accidents happen. The only thing closer to Casey than this emergency bin are his and Lylian's bug-out bags.

The client begins to fidget, he can't keep his focus on the spectacle in front of him. He looks to the television, then to the table lamp, then back to the black screen of the TV. He actively works at fixating on anything that isn't the redundancy of

Casey eating and eating. There isn't much to distract a person in this by-the-hour room. Perhaps inadvertently, he lands his gaze on the open black duffle at the end of the bed. The stacks of money define the bag's canvas. The stranger's attention sits on the opportunity, hanging there just long enough to visibly concern Lylian.

It starts with a twitch. Her arms uncross and she takes one step forward. Her eyes reach for Casey, but he is lost in his gorge, oblivious to Lylian's subtle just-in-case preparations.

This client could be one of David's thugs. Then again, any human being could: all ethnicities, a child, a senior citizen, religious or agnostic. David is an equal opportunity criminal, a true champion of diversity in the workplace.

Lylian puts a hand on the table lamp, wraps her fingers around its base. If this stranger decides to go rogue, she has all she needs to bash the back of his skull.

There is a mumble. It's enough to break the client's fixation on the bag of cash. He looks back to Casey, but Lylian remains committed.

"Did you say something?" the client asks, the words passing through what is left of his jagged, flaxen teeth.

Casey struggles to form a comprehensible answer. His response works its way around the saliva-soaked mass he hasn't stopped chewing. "How will the world know you?" he repeats.

"Are you askin' me? You should be telling me."

The loss of confidence in the client's voice doesn't go unnoticed by Lylian. Her grip tightens on the lamp's base.

With his eyes shut tight, Casey goes adrift on his own question. He silently mouths it a few more times. Then, through quivering lips, he repeats it aloud, changing just the last word.

"How will the world know me?"

"How the fuck should I know?" the client spits.

His head swings back toward Lylian. He is seeking reassurance, says "is this guy for real?" without saying it at all. Lylian is lightning quick.

"Míralo!" she barks. "Por Dios, look ahead, let him work through it." The order is firm enough to keep the client from noticing she's armed.

He turns around and growls, "The pretty ones are always cunts, no?"

Casey's eyes offer nothing.

"Hey! Anybody home?" the client asks, waving a hand in front of Casey. He pounds the table. "Are you seeing anything yet? I didn't pay five-fuckin' grand to hear what the hell *you'll* be doing in the future." Bam! His second pound means business; the clatter of jumping silverware and glass resets Casey's focus.

"Almost ready," he says. "To see you, not me, of course."

Casey's upcoming vision will likely be nothing too improbable. A lover penetrating another man's wife, one partner robbing his best friend or partner blind, an inoperable situation for a sister who doesn't pull through. And those hypotheticals are more dramatic than what Casey typically foresees. There is less oomph in the trade of clairvoyance than its mythos tends to portray.

Casey continues eating. He selects each new item from the table in a simple sequence. Salty, sweet, salty, sweet; repeat, repeat, repeat. The only hard-and-fast rule is this: no reading meal begins with anything other than a whole bag of nacho cheese flavored tortilla chips. Brand-name or any other neon-orange dusted knock-off chip can perform the very same important role. America's favorite snack goes in first and comes out last. When the bright flecks wave back at him from the bottom of the toilet, Casey can be certain he has rid his guts of everything he'd just eaten.

A sixteen-inch sausage pizza sits on the table. The cooling oil on its surface glistens in the flickering light of a dozen candles. The cheap glass tubes are the East Coast variety, each featuring a hastily glued graphic of Divino Niño Jesus on its side. The son of God is trying his best to help the pizza maintain its appeal. The pie is right next to the last wedge of what had been a full chocolate cheesecake. Casey grabs for the final piece of the desert and holds it over a feast that would make Edesia nauseous. He gets stuck in the study of it.

Lylian leans to her left while lightly waving at Casey with her available hand. He doesn't budge. She hurls a near silent *for fuck's sake, keep this thing moving* right at him. Nothing. Her eyes refuse to relent. The intensity of her impatience could burn the whole room down. She takes two angry steps that bring her uncomfortably close to the table, lamp still at the ready, barely hidden behind her back.

The client's head starts to cock over his right shoulder, but Casey shoves the whole gelatinous triangle into his already crowded mouth. It's enough to retain the client's attention. Lylian falls back. The stranger inches his chair closer to the table as if he's not completely satisfied with her retreat. He looks up at Casey, there isn't a hint of disgust on his face. At some point, most clients squirm, but this guy's steady suggests he has seen some things.

Casey swallows, closes his eyes, and reaches for the stranger's willing hands.

The money they're making for this reading hardly seems worth Casey's condition. The duffle bag appears chock-full. At some point, five grand more is no longer the difference between life and death.

Minutes pass with Casey saying nothing. The client appears comfortably unaware that anything might be wrong, his hands resting calmly within Casey's firm grip.

By now, Casey should be reeling off the man's future. The remnants of food on the plates, plastic wrappers, and boxes in front of him suggest a caloric intake of five figures, easy. His eyes open, revealing an uncharacteristic panic. Quickly, he looks past the John, tries to find a solution in Lylian.

From under a puckered brow, she doesn't speak, but the message her face conveys is familiar.

Think of me, think of Ruby.

Casey releases the stranger's hands. His fingers tremble over the table as he searches for one more bite to jump-start the vision. He touches an empty basket that reeks of Double Philly Cheesesteak Burger. The matching basket to its side is down to one dry, leftover chili-cheese fry. Casey throws himself into the hunt, nearly hovering over the table. He rifles around empty two-liters, passes up an open bag of bite-sized chocolate bars, then knocks over a bucket of weight gain powder. The dust-up does little to hide his growing anxiety. He swipes at two ten-piece fried chicken boxes. Empty. He turns over the creamy ranch containers the chicken came with, already licked clean.

Revisiting all he has eaten starts the convulsions. The rise and fall from the deep of his throat is audible. His body will only obey his brain for so long. He must decide on another bite quick or there won't be any need for jamming two fingers hard to the back of the tongue later. To put it plainly, the puke wants out and it wants out now.

With the skill of a teenage boy who practices often on his older sister's bra, Casey pops open a sealed box of donut holes with just one hand. The client follows the trajectory of each tiny confection. From the box to Casey's mouth, from the box to Casey's mouth, one donut hole at a time, then two, then three. When the box is empty, Casey reaches for a Twinkie.

That's the snack that breaks the camel's back. The stranger winces, curling his nostrils overtly to punctuate his disgust. He may be upset by what he is seeing or he may be upset because he is starting to suspect the voodoo he paid for isn't real.

"It is time!" Casey dramatically improvises.

Though the client's anticipation is renewed, Lylian's snide huff is huge.

The man takes on a religious posture of prayer, palm-to-palm like a tent over his nose. For the moment, his suspicions appear to fade and he readies himself for his fortune.

Casey doesn't continue. Not in any meaningful way. His left eyelid goes jittery and his legs are visibly trembling underneath the table. He's stuck in a silent umm.

Lylian shakes her head. With a violent one-finger twirl she implores him to wrap things up quickly.

The sharp snap of a plastic safety seal rocks the room like thunder. The client opens his eyes to find Casey chugging a bottle of French Dressing, the way a pledge might inhale it during a night of hazing. The slow coat of soybean oil and high-fructose corn syrup navigating mucous membrane is easy to feel. The grimace on the client is a wish for an end, and when Casey washes the condiment down with a soda, his relief, and theirs, is real.

"There you are," Casey begins.

The client leans into the start of his story.

"The room is packed in people wearing black and—"

"I don't want to know!" the client shouts as he lifts his mass from his chair. His rise is clumsy, and his pronounced gut bumps the table, spilling the remaining food to the floor. He looks bigger for standing. A shirted boulder atop of toothpick legs. His next intention is a mystery, maybe even to himself.

Lylian makes herself an obstacle to the room's exit. Fight or flight. No one moves, but everyone is ready to make one.

"I've changed my mind," the stranger says, struggling to regain some momentary composure. He sounds disgusted and empathetic, embarrassed and regretful. He takes one last look around the room. "Keep the money. You two need it more than me. I've changed my mind and I don't want to know what it is you've seen."

Casey waves Lylian away from her emergency post. The client stumbles past her. He fumbles with the doorhandle, locking and unlocking the deadbolt a handful of times before getting it open. The man never turns back, but he can be heard mumbling *I don't want to know,* over and over again until the metallic thwap of his car door cuts him off. Ignorance is his surest shot at outrunning the fate that awaits him, at least that's what many clients seem to believe.

The motel door shuts on its own. Before Lylian can say a word, Casey is a pinball coming off its plunger. In the bathroom, he kneels over the toilet with a toothbrush jabbed into the back of his throat. The vomit comes easy and the amount of hurl never disturbs when it is your own.

"What the hell was that?" Lylian asks, no trace of concern for the violence at her feet. She bullies over him as he presses harder to evacuate as much of what he'd eaten as possible. When the neon-orange flecks decorate the top of the barf pile settling in the toilet, she knows he's done. "I said, what the hell was that, Casey?"

"What? He panicked," he says, then forces a few dry heaves for good measure. "Don't act like it's the first time a client balked. We've had plenty of chickenshits, let's just be glad this one didn't demand a refund."

Casey grasps for the sink, tries to stand up, but Lylian puts a heavy hand on his shoulder. He pushes into it and his body quivers under her obstruction.

"You know that's not what I mean," she says.

Casey doesn't respond. Resolved to stay in a squat, he nervously picks at the flakes of vomit stuck to the rim.

"It is time?" Lylian mocks. "I've never heard you say that shit before a vision. Not once. What did you see?"

"Please let me up. It's getting late and I want to squeeze in a run."

"I really don't think you should run tonight."

"I'll make it quick, I promise."

Lylian looks to the hand she is using to keep him from standing. "You're too weak to go for a run," she says as she eases her clutch.

Casey doesn't pass on the opportunity. He jumps up, pushes past her, then hurries his way to the one rank armchair at the front of the room. He grabs for the sneakers and sweatshirt neatly tucked beneath it. With one eye on the exit, he wastes no time in lacing up the trainers tight.

Lylian plops down crisscross applesauce next to him.

"You didn't see anything, did you?"

She earnestly tries to temper the bounce of his anxious leg with a gentler hand than the one before.

"Lyl, it will be dark soon. We can talk about what I saw or didn't see when I get back, I promise."

She keeps a light grip on his knee. There's a quiet urgency in her voice. "Just tell me what you saw first. Please. We are in this together, remember?"

She waits patiently for his response, stays quiet to force him to say something. The same woman who looked capable of an execution is a dark flower. No anger in her eyes, no creases or lines that imply dissatisfaction on her face. She is perfection, a practiced mystery.

"Nothing, Lylian. I saw nothing." His admission sounds more like a quick way to get out the door than any real desire to come clean. "Can I get after it already?"

"Like *nothing* nothing, or like nothing because the something you saw happen to that guy in the future wasn't that big of a deal?"

"The former."

"*Nothing* nothing?"

"That's what I said."

"And you're just going to leave?"

Her hand goes heavy again.

"Are you going to let me?"

Lylian takes a deep breath, but the studied attempt at keeping her poise gives way to an unsteady exhalation. The tendons running from her wrist to her knuckles flinch under her skin. Her fingers push deeper into his thigh, just above the knee, and Casey's leg stills.

"Pobrecito, your body can't keep this up," she says with dwindling kindness. "You must know that. At least *tell* me you know that."

"Just a little longer, Lyl."

"Jesus Christ, we've got plenty of money, let's go back and get Ruby and just leave the country already."

Casey is off the chair with zero resistance. She doesn't stand to follow. She looks spent; her energy quiet. Resigned to her squat on the carpet, Lylian watches him jerk at the door before bounding out of the room. As the slow swing of the metal slab begins to separate them, he shouts, "I know what I am and am *not* capable of right now, Lylian. Another month and then we'll go, don't fuck this up for us."

Lylian rushes a response. "Casey, you are the one fucking this up, and only—" but the thick thump and click of the room's door is the last thing he hears.

Subject: CASEY BANKS
Interviewer: [redacted]
Date of Interview: 11/09/2015
CB=Casey Banks, IN=Interviewer

IN: This interview is being recorded. The time is 9:35AM. Good morning, Casey.

CB: Good morning, [redacted].

IN: How are you feeling?

CB: Well enough.

IN: Well enough to have today's conversation?

CB: If it turns out otherwise, I'm sure you'll let me know.

IN: How's your memory of our last conversation?

CB: If you were to quiz me, I would pass.

IN: Have you eaten breakfast?

CB: I've had coffee.

IN: Black?

CB: Black.

IN: I'm sure you already know that extreme starvation and malnutrition can actually shrink the size of your brain—

CB: I don't have brain fog, [redacted]. And yesterday's reading was on fifteen-thousand calories. I would hardly call that extreme starvation.

IN: I'm told you evacuated the entire meal immediately after you reported your vision. Is that not true?

CB: I'm sure some of that fifteen-thousand calories made its way to the small intestine.

IN: You are sounding annoyed this morning.

CB: Don't I always?

IN: More annoyed than normal.

CB: You've had me here for three weeks—

IN: Twenty-seven days.

CB: Fine, almost four weeks. I have read six times, under observation each time. You have interviewed me before and after each of those readings. Have you made any progress?

IN: My role in this research is that of interviewer. We've discussed that. I ask questions around the topics I am given before each of our visits.

CB: "I don't know," would have been an adequate answer.

IN: Okay then. I don't know.

CB: Who gives you those topics?

IN: The team of people trying to help you, of course.

CB: (inaudible)

IN: Could you repeat that?

CB: I'd prefer not to.

IN: Are you considering leaving this facility?

CB: Can I?

IN: You and Lylian can end this research at any time. We've discussed that as well.

CB: I don't believe you.

IN: The door is right there.

CB: (inaudible)

IN: Holding you here against your will would have negative effects on our research.

CB: Okay.

IN: Even just *believing* that you've no choice in the matter may be detrimental to the research too.

CB: I said okay.

IN: So, you accept that you are always free to leave?

CB: I do. I'm tired, that's all.

IN: Would you like to end this interview?

CB: No. No, I'm fine. What are we talking about today?

IN: I want to discuss the vision that led to you having to work for David.

CB: Haven't I already told you about that?

IN: Do you remember sharing that information with me?

CB: Are you looking for inconsistencies?

IN: No one here believes you are lying, Casey.

CB: So at least one of my visions has come to pass then?

IN: I think that's a safe assumption.

CB: But you don't know for sure.

IN: I just ask the questions.

CB: Where do you want me to start?

IN: Wherever you like.

CB: I was reading for Lylian, it was a down week.

IN: A down week?

CB: Down weeks were her idea. At that point, I would read for clients twice a week for two weeks, four readings total. Then, I would take a full seven days off in between the last reading and the next reading to recover. For my health. I wasn't in favor of that schedule. I wanted to make as much money as possible as quickly as possible, but I think she was afraid I would crash and burn. She was right, of course. The down weeks were great. And we were averaging around thirty grand each month, *with* the down week.

IN: And for how many months had you been charging people to perform readings?

CB: Five. Six, maybe.

IN: Had you read for Lylian before that week?

CB: No. That was against the rules.

IN: No personal readings.

CB: So we *have* had this conversation already.

IN: We've discussed that rule before, yes. So, why the change?

CB: Two reasons: practice and for kicks. To see where my soothsaying might be leading us.

IN: Practice?

CB: I wanted to experiment with how deep I could move forward into a readee's timeline. We were making good money selling visions from days to weeks ahead, but I thought we could charge more if we were able to go further into a client's future. By then, my working theory was pretty simple: eat more, see more. Or at least see farther.

IN: How many calories did you consume for the reading you performed on Lylian that first time?

CB: Around eight-thousand.

IN: And how far into her future did you go?

CB: Not very far it turned out.

IN: Eight-thousand calories wasn't enough.

CB: No. It was plenty. I just hadn't figured out how to fast-forward yet. If that makes sense.

IN: So, in your opinion, there is no correlation between how much you eat and how far you can travel on a timeline.

CB: In my opinion, there absolutely is a correlation. The more I eat, the farther down the road I can see. But the act of consuming a shit-ton of food itself doesn't just magically drop me into months away from the present. The higher the calorie count, the longer I can stay in the vision. The longer I stay in the vision, the further I can go.

IN: In one of our previous chats, you told me you'd been at least as far forward as six months. Just how much food would you have to eat to travel that distance?

CB: No. You're not getting it. Let me try again: the time I have to experience the vision is related to the amount of food I consume. Within that time, just how far into the future I see is entirely up to me. It's akin to fast-forwarding a film, that's the best way I can explain it.

IN: In the vision you had while reading for Lylian, you weren't as far forward as you believed, then.

CB: No. I was lingering. But I didn't know it.

IN: Would you share the details of that vision with me?

CB: I found Lylian kneeling next to a man's body. There was a lot of blood. On his face. On her hands. He wasn't dead, but was making some awful sounds. A kind of gurgling moan. Lylian's face was distraught, but not sad. I mean, I might have interpreted the look on her face as sadness, but she picked up the bat lying next to him, stood up, and used it on him repeatedly. Her expression didn't change, until I guess she was certain he was dead. And then, a morbid kind of relief came over her. There was a young girl crying in the corner.

IN: Lylian's daughter?

CB: Yes. Ruby.

IN: How far into Lylian's future had you traveled?

CB: Just days. Look, later on, during my time with David, I made more effort in any vision to find some concrete indication of the date. But there isn't always a desktop calendar sitting around. And people don't check the date on their phone as often as you might hope. In this instance, I made a fucked-up assumption based on the information I had in front of me and my own flawed theory.

IN: What information?

CB: Lylian's hair was shorter, much shorter.

IN: You assumed it was deep into the future because Lylian had gotten a haircut?

CB: I told you it was a fucked-up reason. In my defense, she'd made no mention of wanting to chop most of her hair off. But more than that, I had entered that vision really believing that just the act of eating more would send me further. Weeks, if not months ahead.

IN: And you decided not to tell Lylian what you had seen, correct?

CB: I made up something. A lie. I told her about a perfect bungalow perched amongst swaying palms. I said I saw us, with Ruby, on an island that I couldn't pinpoint.

IN: You told her what you thought she wanted to hear?

CB: She was already so worried about the effects reading might have on me long term. But her idea of the money we needed to make it to that island to start a new life was very different from my own. My target was justifiably larger, she has no real head for numbers. My whole life prior to reading futures for money was making sense of numbers for a paycheck. We were making really good money reading and I didn't want to stop.

IN: Your actual vision was pretty violent. Weren't you at all distraught? Do you think Lylian believed that all you had seen was the perfect bungalow scenario?

CB: As you said, it was what she wanted to hear.

IN: Or what you *wanted* her to hear. Did you have any intention of telling her at some point, given that you thought it was a ways away from happening?

CB: I can't say for sure I would have. It was much easier to pretend what I'd seen was faulty.

IN: Had you had faulty visions prior?

CB: Not to my knowledge, no.

IN: When did Lylian kill Diego?

CB: Two days after that vision. I'd already given her a key to my place. I was in the shower when she just sort of appeared. The first thing I noticed was her new haircut… then the blood on her clothes. Ruby called out to her from the living room sounding distressed. I knew I'd fucked up. I knew she'd just killed someone. And, though it was an odd time to do so, I made note the larger meal hadn't pushed me any deeper into the future than had been typical.

IN: Did you tell her the truth about the vision you'd had two days prior?

CB: Not immediately, no.

IN: You didn't feel obligated to share that you'd foreseen her murdering Diego?

CB: No.

IN: Why not?

CB: What good would it have done?

IN: You felt that ship had sailed.

CB: Exactly. She cleaned up, we put Ruby to bed, and she told me what had happened.

IN: And what *had* happened?

CB: She caught Diego sexually assaulting Ruby.

IN: And who was Diego to Lylian?

CB: A trusted friend. A friend she thought she could trust, I mean.

IN: That's awful. I'm sorry and I can understand.

CB: (inaudible)

IN: Do you want to continue?

CB: I offered to help her deal with Diego's body, but she told me she already had a plan.

IN: Reaching out to David?

CB: When I woke up the next morning, Ruby and Lyl were gone. To some extent, I shut down. I didn't leave the house that week, except to run.

IN: You still went running?

CB: Of course. I always run. If there is anything you should have learned about me by now, it is that.

IN: When did you next see Lylian?

CB: She came back to my apartment three or four days later.

IN: Alone?

CB: She left Ruby with her mother. And she said the situation with Diego—the body, the mess, all of it—had been taken care of.

IN: By David?

CB: By his people, yeah.

IN: David is Ruby's biological father, correct?

CB: Correct.

IN: What did you know about David at that point?

CB: I knew she'd left him. She was hiding from him. I didn't know he was connected to the cartels.

IN: Why do you think David helped Lylian?

CB: She offered to introduce him to a man that could see the future.

IN: And that was okay with you?

CB: Anything for love, right? Virginia Anne is most certainly rolling in her grave.

IN: Didn't it seem odd to you David would make that deal?

CB: At the time, maybe.

IN: Surely, he didn't actually believe he was about to meet a legitimate psychic?

CB: Who can say? But I've since learned that David has a pretty open mind when it comes to anything that might enrich him, no matter how half-cocked the idea sounds.

IN: And so, you agreed to read futures, for David—

CB: It wasn't presented to me as a choice.

IN: In the vision you had of Lylian killing Diego, had you seen Diego sexually assaulting Ruby?

CB: God no. Had I seen that, I'd have told Lylian.

IN: Did you ask Ruby if she'd been sexually assaulted?

CB: No.

IN: Why not?

CB: That's not something you ask a five-year-old.

IN: I don't think you believe that.

CB: I know what you are insinuating, but he did do it.

IN: Because Lylian told you he did it.

CB: (inaudible)

IN: You lied to Lylian about what you saw, but—

CB: But what?

IN: Well, I have to ask: how can you be sure that she killed
Diego for that reason?

2

_____

He is a speck.

Casey is on the move, miles away from the motel and hours past the regrettable way he left things with Lylian. Outside of the room, he'd stopped, then waited as he ran in place. But when the door didn't reopen, Casey accelerated into a run that is still going.

He races through the thick of a plaza. Squalor overwhelms a hasty attempt at gentrification made many years prior. The buildings, some vacant, some metal splintering from stone, are the color of a forgotten promise. Bleached into a con long ago. If the town had a heyday, it is two decades to the wind, but not entirely uninhabited.

Midstride, Casey reaches deep into the kangaroo pocket of his hoodie for a phone he left behind. Moderate irritation escapes his face with a *fuck*. Casey isn't looking for stimulus to keep his mind off the grind. He is counting seconds between objects at distances that are easy to work out, then plugging that information into calculations to give him some idea of his pace and the calories he burns. With no GPS, no running apps in hand, years of experience will have to do.

From behind hard metal security cages, storefront windows beckon. He starts a noticeable deviation from the road. The imperfections and warps of shoddy industrial glass will make for a less than ideal reality check, but he guides himself closer to the sidewalk along the mall. After all, a man with no idea of how he looks is a man with no idea of what to feel. To be fair, the diffused light of overcast skies is one hell of a drug. A flattering reflection might just be possible on a day like this. Without slowing, he catches a glimpse of his haggard condition, then bounds back to the street just as quickly as he'd left.

The air is thick with salt. The beachfront lies ahead, and the breeze off the ocean is thankfully pushing the rank smell of uncollected garbage to Casey's rear. He takes in deeper breaths, but the relief he feels is short-lived.

An unmarked black Chevy Tahoe approaches behind Casey, matching his pace. The safety of the salt-washed flats on the other side of the dunes is close, but not close enough. The vehicle passes him, then stops in between Casey and the busted boardwalk ahead. What few witnesses there were have retreated into the dark shadows they rely on. Casey slows until he's running in place.

With the SUV idling ten feet in front of him, he evaluates the narrow spaces of abutted buildings. Each escape route comes with its own back-alley obstacles. A sprint seems imminent, but Casey is too late to commit. The Tahoe's tinted rear passenger window drops. From within, a hulk-like head atop of a fleshy tree trunk emerges.

"Should I have Jim park the car? I'd be happy to finish up the run with you, Casey."

Despite his mass, he springs from the vehicle.

Casey doesn't wait for him to catch up.

Maybe it is the effect of deserted streets, but his new running buddy's occupancy outdoors is truly impressive. The stranger is a billboard of genetic perfection: six-foot-three, no feature left unchiseled, thinning hair that pretends well at being a full head of hair, and a swagger that can't be learned.

He makes it to Casey's side, breathing heavy already.

"You look gooooood, Casey." His sarcasm is thick and unrefined. "You put on some weight?"

"Fuck off, Cooper."

"What mile are we on?"

"Sixteen."

"Impressive. Try to keep your throw-up off my shoes."

Five minutes pass and neither man says a word. As they run over the remains of an Atlantic White Cedar boardwalk, the repetitive pounding of four feet matching strides is hypnotic. Casey is untroubled. For a moment, he finds serenity within his predicament. Cooper takes note.

"So," Cooper says, shattering the meditative moment, "surprised I found you?"

Casey slows his pace to something more accommodating for conversation.

"Surprised it took you so long, if I'm being honest."

Cooper's fist lands swiftly. The punch to Casey's face was made with half the force available to the man who threw it. Casey manages to keep his footing. His ambivalence to the attack suggests it isn't the first time Cooper's slugged him. The recovery is quick and their pace doesn't suffer for the assault.

"Why'd the two of you bolt?" Cooper asks. "I thought my instructions were pretty fuckin' simple."

"They were, and we didn't run from you. Not exactly."

"You weren't where I told you to be, I know that. You weren't there the next day either, or the next day… Where were you hiding?"

"We weren't *hiding* from you."

Another thwack. Cooper's second jab has more power, more knuckle too. This wallop sends Casey careening toward the dunes, still on his feet, but searching for balance as his trainers sink into the deep sand to the side of the boardwalk. He goes up and down the knolls, returning to the planks with only a slight dent in their speed.

"Casey, we don't have time for this shit. Did you go back to David's? Who helped you disappear? I don't mean to sound like a shithead, but I'm having a hard time believing you and Lylian could just go click-click poof on your own."

Cooper's increasing volume grabs the attention of one lonely man, an aged treasure-seeker mining the beach with an ancient metal detector. He looks away as quickly as he'd taken note, cinches the shoulder sack holding his haul, returns his attention to anything but none of his business.

"We had no intention of blowing you off," Casey insists as he steadies himself for another punch. "You left the bar. Per your instructions, Lylian and I hung around there for a while longer. Then, some other guy shows up. He looks the part."

"Looks the part of what?" Cooper asks with a snarl.

"He looked exactly like the kind of asshole that an asshole like you would work with."

While remaining in motion, Casey's preps his upper body to absorb more punishment, but no punch comes.

"It's in your best interest to start getting specific."

"He introduced himself as Ben Walsh. Was that his real name? Hell if I know. But he said he was aware of my talents. Told me there was a secure location ready for us. And if we wanted his help, the only option was to leave with him immediately."

"Your *talents?*"

"His words, not mine."

"You really don't think much of me, do you?" Cooper asks.

Before Casey can answer, Cooper snatches him by his collar and yanks him into a complete stop.

Casey puts his hands to bent knees, then peers up at his

assailant from the crouch. The question was clearly rhetorical, but Casey's agitation is more evident than his fear.

"Not true. From the day we first met you, I've always thought you were a very handsome man."

A third punch flies, softer than the first two, but Cooper lands it perfectly between Casey's upper lip and septum. This hit stuns. Casey keeps his feet under himself, but there is no hiding the troubling sway of everything above his waist. He runs a thumb along the teeth still clinging to his upper jaw. The blood on its tip is thick, the viscosity unsettling. His daze gives way to panic, then panic turns quickly to nausea. Vomit looks certain. Casey blinks frenetically as he erects himself, swallowing hard. He points in the direction they'd been running and Cooper agrees to the ask. Both men leap back into the run.

"I'm gonna level with you, Casey. Any more mention of your I-can-see-the-future bullshit, and I'm gonna stop going light on you. But, let's say for a minute that I buy your story. You didn't think to ask this guy if he was with me? If he knew me? If he was part of the plan I'd so carefully constructed and clearly articulated to you both?"

For a moment, Cooper's mood goes reasonable.

"I asked if the safehouse was a part of your plan."

"And?"

Casey hesitates. "There was a nod."

"You fucked up my plan on a nod?" Cooper shouts. The sudden outburst draws the attention of a family of four. The clan reeks of having been hoodwinked into vacationing here. Nothing about their reaction suggests either parent plans on intervening. But just in case, Casey lowers his volume, returns it to a hush.

"Cooper, I'm not trying to be difficult, but…"

"But what?"

"You had *nothing* to do with it?" Casey asks. "The whole time, I was never entirely sure."

Cooper's attention is elsewhere. He's got his eye on a group of youths under a pier up ahead. If they give a fuck about the approaching pair, they show no signs of it. As Casey and Cooper pass under the abandoned landing, one of the kids babbles, "Yo, runner guy." Casey acknowledges their loose connection with a quick raised brow. The odd interaction brings Cooper out of threat-assessment mode.

"Friends of yours?"

"This isn't my first run out here."

Cooper leaves his concern behind.

"You didn't think it was odd when I never showed up at wherever the fuck you were?"

"I asked for you, I asked about you."

"Sure, you did," Cooper sneers. "Where were they holding you?"

"They weren't holding us. Lylian and I were free to go whenever. And we did go… when I had finally seen enough."

"Fine," Cooper says. "That's what this operation let you believe. Where were they *not* holding you, then?"

"I don't know."

"You don't know," Cooper repeats.

"My best guess would be Nevada, California, New Mexico, Mexico maybe, or just some part of Arizona far away from Tucson."

"That's some best guess, Casey. Jesus Christ."

"We were in the back of a van with no windows. There were multiple stops. Gas or who knows what. I'm just saying it was a long ride there and a long ride back."

"When did these fine people let you leave?"

"A few weeks ago."

"In the back of a van again, I take it. With no windows?"

"Yep."

"Of course."

The boardwalk disappears behind them. Under their feet, a

quarter mile of runnable beach gives way to freshly soaked sand. Casey waits on Cooper to pick-up the conversation again. The rising tide leaves them with no choice but to dart up a natural stone staircase and back onto the road that hugs the edge of the town. Once on the pavement, they round a corner into the square. The pitch of Casey's motel roof is just shy of a mile ahead of them.

The street-lamps flicker. For every one that dutifully illuminates, two others refuse. The second-floor windows of the buildings they pass feature far more shadows and silhouettes than the hour before. Some of the shapes are clearly watching the two out-of-towners, jogging through the neighborhood as if it were their own.

Cooper breaks what had been a nice silence, "I need names."

"I can't be sure that any of the names they used were real."

"I don't give a fuck, just give me whatever names they gave you."

"Fine," Casey agrees as he subtly changes the direction of their run. "I'll put those together."

He turns toward a new street that leads out of the square. If Cooper cooperates, they won't pass Casey's motel any time soon.

"So, these fake-name fucks dump you off where, then?"

"Back in Tucson."

"And why didn't you look for me then?"

"Honestly?"

"No, dipshit, lie to me."

"Lylian got it into her head you were working for David. That you were his quiet way of bringing us back to him."

"And you?"

"Me? I've just never cared for your company."

Wham. Cooper's fist is vicious this time. It drives into Casey's sternum, impels him into the cracked asphalt below. Casey barely brings himself back into a squat. He's been bit by the street. He wipes away blood from the separated skin over his knee, then looks up, tries to find Cooper in the day's last light.

"You can't be this dumb," Cooper says with a wheeze. He's huffing and puffing now.

Casey enjoys Cooper's pain, sneaks out the tiniest of smiles.

"Scratch that," Cooper continues. "Maybe you've always been this fucking dumb."

He holds out an arm toward the ground, pulls Casey up, then watches as his victim immediately pulls away. Cooper's face seems genuinely contrite.

When Casey finds a perimeter that exists just outside of Cooper's gorilla-like reach, he asks, "Are you actually a federal agent or just some asshole pretending to be?"

Cooper doesn't answer. Waves crashing blends with the jukebox tunes wafting from the dive-bar still in business. Casey studies the sour all over Cooper's face. He could be contemplating all this new information, or he might be genuinely winded.

"Kick his ass!"

"My money's on the giant!"

The two men are no longer alone. The shouts are many, but flimsy.

"Are you going to answer me?" Casey asks.

Cooper starts and stops a reply, as if his answer is trapped in his face.

"Did you read while you were at this place?" Cooper asks. "What I mean is, did these people want you to read the future for them?"

"I did. They did. It was research."

"And you never thought to try to bounce over to my timeline? Didn't see me in your own?"

"That wasn't what they assigned, I—"

"Never went looking into Ruby's future?"

Cooper reaches into his pocket and pulls out a clover-patterned handkerchief sopped in sweat. He passes it over to Casey. The kindness catches him off guard, giving Cooper's last question time to settle.

"Ruby? Why are you asking about Ruby?"

"Jesus Christ, Casey. This whole thing was going to be a whole hell of a lot easier before you two disappeared. Wherever you were or weren't, it doesn't matter now."

"I'm not making it up, Cooper."

"Listen to me, will ya? David has Ruby now. And that shit is on you. That shit is on both of you."

Subject: CASEY BANKS
Interviewer: [redacted]
Date of Interview: 11/13/2015
CB=Casey Banks, IN=Interviewer

IN: This interview is being recorded. The time is 2:35PM. Good afternoon, Casey.

CB: Hello, [redacted].

IN: How are you feeling today? One to ten?

CB: Good enough.

IN: Is sleep an issue for you? Now or in the past?

CB: It's too hot in here to sleep.

IN: It does feel warm. You have control of the room's thermostat. Would you like to adjust it now? Maybe lose the sweatshirts?

CB: No. I'll figure out the right balance.

IN: You are scheduled to read again tomorrow. Do upcoming readings give you anxiety?

CB: Has the team figured out a way for me to read without binge-eating?

IN: I don't believe so.

CB: Then yeah, I've some trepidation.

IN: About eating though, not what you'll see?

CB: The subject timelines the team has assigned so far have been relatively pedestrian. So, unless that is about to change, no, I can't say I worry much about what future I might see.

IN: What about the readings David had you perform? There must have been some anxiety before each of those.

CB: At first, yes. But eventually, I became numb to it. It is easier than you think to shrink the importance of your role in the murder of men and women when they are criminals. Those people knew the dangers of their chosen profession. Plus, it's not like David was brining those subjects to his house to kill them in front of me.

IN: What exactly was David having you look into?

CB: People that worked for him.

IN: Their futures?

CB: What they were doing in the future, yes.

IN: Why?

CB: To see if they were being loyal to him or fucking him over.

IN: I'm trying to follow—

CB: I'll make it super simple for you: David would give me a subject, I'd go into their timeline to see if they were skimming or committing some other criminal infidelity and then report back to him.

IN: And David would kill them before they could commit these supposed betrayals?

CB: No, no. Not at first.

IN: Go on.

CB: In the beginning, he waited to see if the double-dealings or fuckups I was witnessing would actually come to pass.

IN: How many times did he give his people the benefit of the doubt?

CB: I don't know, six, seven maybe. He needed proof that what I was seeing was legitimate. And when each one of those individuals finally fucked up, as I had foreseen, David removed them.

IN: By murdering them.

CB: Well, yeah. But to his credit, once he no longer doubted the validity of what I was seeing, he genuinely tried to interfere on some of their behalves.

IN: David thought he could alter their futures?

CB: Wouldn't you?

IN: I assume he couldn't.

CB: I have no idea. Maybe he had changed a timeline or two, but ultimately decided that any one of those people would likely be disloyal to him further down the road.

IN: You are saying they were destined to betray him at some point?

CB: I'm saying maybe David felt that way.

IN: What do you believe?

CB: I don't think you can undo your future. Not in any meaningful way.

IN: You don't subscribe to free will, then?

CB: I have no evidence that it exists.

IN: Are you suggesting that whatever you see in a vision is guaranteed to happen? In some form or another?

CB: I can tell you this: I really, really hope that is not the case.

IN: Have you seen something that you are hoping to alter?

CB: Short of maybe locking someone in a room permanently, I don't currently think that radical changes can be made to any subject's fate.

IN: Are you here to test that theory?

CB: I am here to learn. But, yes, I am also hiding here. In a manner of speaking.

IN: Is hiding here working?

CB: It's not that black and white, [redacted]. You should ask the team to put altering someone's future on their research to-do list. Let them test it out.

IN: For all I know, that's already part of this study.

CB: Well, please share those results with me if and when they become available.

IN: Are you afraid of David?

CB: Now? No.

IN: Did you resist reading for him at first?

CB: No.

IN: But not because you were afraid of him?

CB: It's such a thin line between respect and fear. For me at least, probably genetic.

IN: How often did you read for David?

CB: Two times a week for two weeks, with one week off in between.

IN: So, the same rules you and Lylian created.

CB: At first, yes.

IN: Aside from being at least partially responsible for the torture and deaths of many of David's employees, how was it there?

CB: (inaudible)

IN: What was that?

CB: It didn't suck.

IN: He treated you well?

CB: Everyone who we came into contact with treated us well. And David's house is like something from MTV's *Cribs*.

IN: The show about celebrity homes?

CB: That's the one.

IN: So, I gather there was a lot to keep you entertained?

CB: Tons. It had a bowling alley, for Christ's sake. Decked out as if it were a standalone joint. Neon, a bar, retro videogames lining the walls. There was even a guy working the shoe rental counter, at least anytime we were there. I imagine he had other jobs too.

IN: Are you a big bowler?

CB: No. Not in the slightest, I'm just saying. There was a library, movie theater, more than one pool, and we were waited on hand and foot.

IN: Because Lylian was David's ex?

CB: Maybe. Or maybe when my visions materialized, his people didn't want to get on my bad side.

IN: And Lylian was happy there too?

CB: Less so, but she could take the jet to and from Arizona to see Ruby every other weekend. She didn't hate the lifestyle she'd left behind, she hated the man and what he did to provide it.

IN: Were you able to go with her to visit Ruby?

CB: No.

IN: And that didn't bother you?

CB: Of course it did. But I put those weekends to good use.

IN: Doing what?

CB: Running mostly. In the gym, around the property. It all sounds kind of fucked-up, doesn't it?

IN: That's not for me to say.

CB: You don't have to, in hindsight, I can say confidently that it was fucked-up.

IN: In a week-one interview, you told me that vomiting has nothing to do with your ability to see the future. Do you still believe that?

CB: Of course I do. It is a fact.

IN: So, you don't have to puke to have a vision?

CB: Puking came later. The puking was personal. I had read successfully without puking countless times, at David's and before we went to David's too. Vomiting became necessary when I realized that running on its own, no matter the distances I logged, was no longer nullifying the food intake required to have a vision.

IN: Even now, you are confident your bulimia hasn't become a critical aspect of the process?

CB: Why? Is there data that suggests otherwise?

IN: Not that I'm aware.

CB: Well, I don't plan on stopping.

IN: When did you add evacuation?

CB: Two months into working for David.

IN: You'd never practiced bulimia? Prior to meeting Lylian? Prior to developing this ability?

CB: I wasn't anti-bulimia. There is a great fictional upside that can be charming. As an anorexic, I ate only what I needed. There is a real discipline to that, I can assure you. As a bulimic, I imagined I might be able to experience foods I hadn't had in years and be able to do so without consequences.

IN: But you never tried it?

CB: The mortality rate for men my age who practice both eating disorders is fourteen times greater than the norm, but I gather you are aware of that.

IN: I am.

CB: Well, I have never been actively trying to die.

IN: When you made the decision to be both anorexic and bulimic, had you actually put on any additional weight?

CB: It's unlikely that sixteen new ounces to a frame like mine would be noticeable to anyone other than me and a Tanita BC-558 Ironman.

IN: That is a scale?

CB: It is a segmental body composition analyzer.

IN: That you had brought with you to David's?

CB: That David's people bought me, day one.

IN: You were one pound heavier than your target weight and—

CB: There's no actual target weight, [redacted], just a balance. The goals I set for myself shift. Contrary to popular belief, I am not always trying to lose weight. I am trying to achieve a certain balance.

IN: Okay. So, one day, at David's, you became aware of this new pound and then you just committed to throwing up?

CB: You're acting like one pound isn't a big deal.

IN: I understand *you* think it is a big deal.

CB: It's a funny thing, weight.

IN: How so?

CB: On an average body, one pound just blends with the others. Five pounds can blend even.

IN: But with you?

CB: It's like a pimple on a perfect face. No one wants to wait for a pimple to leave on its own schedule. They want it gone. Immediately. There are whole grocery store aisles stocked with cheats to handle that blemish, and no one buying those products is considered disordered.

IN: You can't throw-up a pound, Casey.

CB: I tried to run it off, trust me. I added five more miles a day to my run.

IN: How many runs a week?

CB: Six.

IN: And you didn't lose that pound?

CB: I did. But I knew there'd be others, and it turns out that at my age, the ligaments, muscles, cartilage, and bones in a body can only absorb so much.

IN: You decided to add throwing-up as a precaution? For future pounds?

CB: David brought in a sport's doctor. He was a physical therapist of sorts, and that helped some. He offered me painkillers, but I declined.

IN: Why?

CB: Throwing up was the only way forward.

IN: Had you seen a heavier version of yourself in a vision?

CB: I didn't have to. Do the math.

IN: I'll be honest, I'm a little frustrated right now, Casey. I don't think you are answering my questions.

CB: Eat to see, see to live.

IN: But not if it means getting fat?

CB: I'd rather be dead.

IN: (inaudible)

CB: Each new reading was requiring more and more eating. More calories to activate. And it didn't matter how short or far a distance in time I was being asked to foresee, I needed to eat more to see at all.

IN: Reducing the number of readings, stopping them altogether, these weren't considerations? Were you afraid to ask for a break?

CB: Probably. But bigger meals render more details. Bigger meals lead to more time in the vision itself. And those bigger meals are only a possibility with bulimia.

IN: (inaudible)

CB: I understand how disturbing it is for me to basically cop to giving the barbaric practice a legit reason for being.

IN: At some point, we'd like for you to perform a reading and then refrain from throwing up directly after.

CB: Why?

IN: As a baseline.

CB: I can't say that I will agree to that.

IN: I'm only asking for you to consider it.

CB: Not likely.

IN: If Lylian asked you to try and read without puking, would you?

CB: This is all temporary. All of this.

IN: The puking or the readings?

CB: Both.

IN: You believe you'll stop puking and stop reading?

CB: I believe there's an end.

IN: You've seen that?

CB: I am just saying that I can't read forever.

IN: Certainly not as an anorexic-bulimic.

CB: Yeah. Certainly not.

IN: What made you decide to try to escape from David's?

CB: On an off week, I performed an unscheduled reading.

IN: On who?

CB: On myself.

IN: And what did you see?

3

He is timid.

Like a beaten animal, Casey crosses over the threshold of the motel door. He wills his aching body inside, where his safety feels deeply uncertain.

The post-run stink on his clothes does little to mute the wash of infected molecules exiting the room. The space feels darker than he left it. Its oppression more amplified now that the sun has moved on. Four hours later and the room still pulsates with his and Lylian's mutual frustration.

Just two steps in, Casey freezes. The door seals his fate, emphatically fastening an oversized lap bolt into its frame. The sound startles him, nearly bringing him out of his shoes. The thick click echoes unhampered about the room's vinyl walls. The reverberations are lonely. It is all the attestation needed to realize that Lylian is not there waiting for him.

The feast has been removed. The boxes, containers, lids, bags, and sets of plastic cutlery have been dutifully trashed elsewhere. There are lavender-scented candles burning, but they are now just the ends of lit wicks in pools of liquified wax, scheming to start fires. Every available outlet has been stuffed with a plug-in freshener, the electrically boiled fragrances don't match. Carpet powder rises around each step Casey takes into the room. The tiny piles of chemically infused baking soda do their best to release a fresh scent, but only when disturbed. In their battle against the stench of Casey's work, all of the products have failed miserably.

The two bug-out bags have been placed alongside the monied duffle at the end of an expertly made-up bed.

"Lyl?" Casey asks, his eyes still on the bags, "Lyl, are you in the bathroom?"

Each bag is stuffed, but unzipped and wide open. There looks to be no money missing from the bigger bag. Inside the two others, three-day rotations of his and hers clothing are rolled tight in and around various toiletries. Casey spots a small black flip-phone tucked snug into Lylian's bag. He puzzles over it, reaches slowly toward it as if it were a wounded mouse still capable of delivering a ferocious bite.

A dull thump from the rear of the room shifts his attention.

The bathroom door is shut. He approaches it uneasily, then gently knocks twice on the hollow-core slab. There is no answer from the other side. Inchmeal, he opens it. His face is that of a child making the last few nerve-racking turns of a jack-in-the-box's crank. The door opens wide enough to unhide even someone as diminutive as Lylian. It is unoccupied, and for the first time since reentering their room, Casey lets out a breath that could be classified as an exhale.

With the exception of the missing mirror over the vanity, the bathroom looks better prepared for guests than it had when he'd left. The clean rectangle imprint is calling to him from over the sink. There is no reflection where his reflection should be.

He pulls his sweatshirt off and loses himself in a familiar stance of self-examination, no mirror necessary. The sweat-soaked tee clinging to his torso features blood in various states of consistency. It comes up and over his head with an expected degree of difficulty. The deep pains buried under violent abrasions has Casey moving gingerly. He tosses the sullied shirt into the tub, then cocks his head down, putting his chin to his chest to peer down at his body. He runs a hand lightly over a few ribs that look ready to burst through the skin. His abdomen is holding its own, flat and unyielding to the fat surely trying to find it. He prods at the new cuts, scrapes, and bruises. Some of the lesions are still wet, some have dried. He compiles the details of his physical form, measuring the sum of himself. Concern jumbled with misguided pride, Casey wears the hybrid-feeling as well as ever. A self-induced trance that holds his attention tight. It is all the distraction required to allow Lylian to slip through the bathroom door undetected.

"What took you so long?" she asks him, close enough to be his shadow, soft enough to be in his head. Casey turns to her quickly. Her voice is calm. The exasperation from earlier is no longer a part of her tone. "Long for you, anyway."

Holding his breath, he presents himself, showcasing more than a few new stigmata. Lylian's face is stoic and unflinching. The open gash on his cheek is unmissable. Purple and black bruises litter his head to his forearms. All the gory details to corroborate any story he might choose to tell are there, but none of his visible suffering conjures the empathy he wishfully anticipates.

"Did someone jump you?" There isn't the tiniest uptick of concern in her tone. "Take a big fall?"

If she's at all bothered by Casey's latest reinvention, it is chillingly unobvious. Her ambivalence deflates him and he shuffles his limbs into a subservient pose. From there, he whispers in a timbre that implies don't-shoot-the-messenger.

"Cooper is here," he says.

Lylian doesn't blink. "Of course, he is." She spins away from him before her irritation is visible. "I knew we were pushing our luck."

She creates as much distance from Casey as the room will allow, then turns to face him.

"I begged you, do you remember me begging you right after we'd left David's to just bounce, to leave with what we had?" She leans unsteadily against a dresser pockmarked with a decade of cigarettes' kisses. "How the fuck, Casey? How?"

He festers in indecision and balances himself over the bathroom's doorsill. "I have no idea," he says, looking to the bags at the end of the bed. He eyes the flip-phone. "Who even knows we're here?"

The question teeters on the edge of accusation. The insinuation is loud and clear, but for the moment, she remains unignited.

"My mom wouldn't tell that pendejo anything. And, if that's what you're suggesting, this cool and calm moment I'm trying to have with you will be short-lived as fuck."

"Under normal circumstances, I'd agree with you."

"Casey, who told Cooper we were here?" Lylian asks again.

"He didn't say exactly."

Lylian pops from against the dresser. With just one firm step forward, her bearing on the room is instantly more potent. It's the product of insistence that outweighs the woman by five-fold.

Casey walks out of the bathroom, steps toward the bags, extends a hand toward a clean shirt. "Cooper didn't know anything about the research—"

"This is the last time I'm asking politely, Casey. How did Cooper find us?"

Casey says nothing. He freezes in the pause Lylian has allowed. It's the kind of standstill ripe for the creation of a lie. Against the final ticks of a bomb that can't be defused, sometimes, the truth spills before a man can fashion the lie meant to replace it.

"Your mom, Lylian," Casey confesses. "Like it or not, it was your mom that told Cooper we were here."

"You motherfucker," she shouts. The distance between them evaporates instantly. She forces a petite but powerful index finger repeatedly into the sunken cavity between two naked ribs. Jab after jab is made in an unsound attempt to punctuate her rebuke. Each pointed stab drives deeper and deeper as if she believes the action itself is the key to reversing their course.

"She wouldn't do that. She. Wouldn't. Do. That!"

Casey absorbs every blow. His footing stays firm.

"I know she wouldn't," he says as he waits for an end to her assault. "I know you think she wouldn't... unless she had to."

The rhythm of her plunging finger turns into a barrage of open-handed cracks to his bare torso. When the hammering doesn't subside, he reaches around her, wraps all he has left about her flailing limbs to contain them. Tears pool in her eyes as she fights to deny full-acceptance of what Casey has left unsaid.

"Lyl—"

"Don't you fucking say it, Casey," she says.

"I'm sure I don't have to."

She explodes away from him, bursting the myth of his comfort. The force of her rejection is enough to put him off balance, sends him backward and into the room's rear wall.

"Don't you fucking say it!"

Casey surrenders to what is necessary.

"David has Ruby, Lylian," he says. "I'm sorry."

Her shriek is immediate. There are few sounds in the natural world as debilitating as the howl of a mother, human or animal, who has lost her young to a predator. Lylian's screams of pain are accompanied by a cacophony of blistering crashes. What little is available for destruction is obliterated against the walls. An ashtray, the remote, another ashtray, the single-serving coffee pot; the falling pieces of one item hardly make it to the floor before her destruction of the next. If there are neighbors occupying other rooms within one-hundred feet, there will certainly be phone calls. And if there are phone calls, there will certainly be police. Her ire leaves no opening for Casey to outline next-steps or to say anything that might quell her anguish.

Over a seemingly unending agony, Casey says, "Cooper has a new plan." His volume is of no consequence. His words miss the target, and she doesn't respond. "Lylian," he shouts, "you have to listen to me!"

The momentum of her outpouring fades. It has little to do with his well-intentioned interruption, there is simply nothing left to liquidate. She drops her body hard into a wall opposite Casey, guiding herself to a slump on the floor. Her hands are at her head, exhausted from the fight and trembling over her eyes. Then, as if someone had mistakenly hit mute, she is quiet.

Casey says nothing.

Slowly, there are signs of a self-induced return to composure. She works a pattern to her breathing. She sits still.

"Look. Cooper will be here soon. We need to get on the same page," Casey says as he sets the TV remote's innards onto the bedside table. "We need to present a unified front."

Lylian brings her arms to her sides. The sorrow and anger that had perverted every part of her expression is reborn as steadfast resolution. Her eyes are demanding answers from above thick black smears of mascara, she is more warrior than hapless captive. After taking inventory of the leveling she has caused, she cocks her peer towards Casey. There is zero wiggle room in the compromise she offers.

"No. We've got to go now, Casey, and I mean now. Fuck Cooper. And fuck his plan. The old one and the new one."

She returns to her feet and pulls a clean shirt for Casey from his bag. He is stuck in processing her desire to put Cooper in their rearview. She delicately pulls the garment over his head and onto his torso. All business. Resistance to her momentum would be a fool's errand, but Casey is happy to apply.

"Lylian, I don't think this ends well for us if we don't at least try to work with Cooper."

"I didn't trust him before, I don't know why you expect me to trust him now."

With her back to him, she forces the zippers over all the two bug-out bags hold. She reaches for the duffle and brings the three bags' straps over one shoulder. Casey reaches out for her hand. Surprisingly, perhaps to them both, Lylian doesn't refuse the gesture.

"I've never trusted him either. Not completely," Casey says. His agreement sounds forced. "But I think we have a better shot with him than without him. He isn't alone this time and I'd say he is motivated. Very. Even if helping us is just the byproduct of him using us to help himself—"

"God you're dumb," she capitulates.

Though her anger has been relit, she gently releases his hand. He immediately tries to still her, grabs her shoulders to turn her around. She is not easily manhandled. He can sense the vast chasm between his and her physical strength. Lylian is armed with an otherworldly capability: a power exclusive to a mother with only one focus. She is stone in his hands, and he removes his grip. He backpedals his way toward the door. She watches Casey ready himself for one last stand, more nuisance than obstacle. For a moment, she is charmed, but the emerald twinkle goes dark.

"Casey, where is my mother?"

He can't look her in the eye. He catches his reflection in the television's dark screen. It reveals a murky representation of a man whose posturing is useless. There are no specific details, but his ineptitude is crystal clear.

"Casey, where is my mom?" she asks again.

With zero hesitation, Lylian bends to pick up what's left of a lamp. With it firmly in hand, she raises its jagged nickel base toward him. Casey understands the threat's validity.

"Listen: any minute now, Cooper is going to be at that door," he insists. "And if you give him—if you give us—a minute to explain, I think you'll see how our chances of getting Ruby, getting your mom, getting them both, are much better with Cooper than they are if we just go rogue. We can't do this alone, Lylian, think about it!"

Lylian moves closer to him.

He puts his hands in front of himself, a halfhearted attempt at a defense, one that suggests he doesn't actually think he'll need it.

"Casey, please believe me when I say this is for your own good."

The lamp is up and back quick, it strikes like lightning. She rakes its base across the crown of his skull just above his right temple. There is a troubling liquid crack. The hit is all his body needs to fumble and fold itself into a disturbing arrangement upon the floor. He is immobile. His eyes work hard to stay in the fight, look for her help from behind short-circuiting lids.

"God dammit, Casey," Lylian says. "I didn't want to do that." The lamp drops from her hands, creating one last crash. "I shouldn't have *had* to do that."

She drops herself onto the bed. She pulls her bag from her shoulder, then frantically unzips it while keeping watch over Casey. She finds the flip-phone and opens it quickly. She punches at keys, writes a message as fast as the T9 text can translate it. She hits send, smacks the black clamshell shut, and tosses the device back into her bag before sealing it tight. When she has all three bags securely over her shoulders again, she stands to leave.

"This isn't what I wanted," she says. With one foot on either side of him, bags dangling uncooperatively, Lylian squats to cup a hand to his face. "Not at all how I hoped things would go when I introduced you to David. And for that, I'm sorry." She tugs a single packet of tightly stacked one-hundred-dollar bills from the duffle, lays the money next to his head. "I'm as much to blame as you are for the clusterfuck this has become. Maybe more so. At some point, I'll try to make that right with you, but now is not the time."

Lylian opens the door and the wet ocean air swims its way through the darkness. It is a welcome reprieve, but falls short of motivating Casey to move. With a solid grip on the doorknob, she turns around to address him once more. She is angry, she is sorry, she is angry, she is sorry, seemingly stuck in the formation of a final goodbye that she can't decide upon.

Behind her, the black Tahoe crawls into the parking lot. Casey tries to lift himself from the floor, but his arm buckles under his weight. He mutters a warning, too faint to be heard over the apology Lylian begins.

"Baby, I'm sorry—"

There's a thick slap of muddled flesh. One pop from Cooper and Lylian crashes down into Casey. It knocks the wind from his lungs. Her body lies motionless, resting atop his. The injury on the rear of her head adds fresh red warmth to the crusted remnants of Casey's blood. Cooper's shadow engulfs them both as Casey struggles to keep his eyes open.

"Fucking amateur hour in here," Cooper says to the imposing shapes following him into the room. "Get these two dipshits cleaned up and prepped for the plane."

Subject: CASEY BANKS
Interviewer: [redacted]
Date of Interview: 11/23/2015
CB=Casey Banks, IN=Interviewer

IN: This interview is being recorded. The time is 10:15AM. Good morning, Casey.

CB: Good morning.

IN: How was your week off from reading?

CB: Uneventful.

IN: This facility's perks must pale in comparison to those you enjoyed at David's.

CB: We'll manage.

IN: I imagine seeing other people's futures is very stimulating. Perhaps you now find the present to be boring.

CB: Most of the futures I have seen are far from titillating. It turns out humanity has done a bang-up job of keeping most of itself on a pretty predictable hamster wheel.

IN: Perhaps, but I find the recordings of the futures you report to be unique, in and of themselves.

CB: You should probably get out more.

IN: It's true the timelines we've put you on here have not been blockbusters. But there is something odd about the way you deliver the information, there's just so many details. I often feel like I'm listening to you read a book.

CB: Well, all great psychics have their gimmick.

IN: In that what it is? Your narration style? A gimmick?

CB: Partly, yeah. I mean if you can't tell someone that something amazing is going to happen to them, the least you can do for five grand is create the most interesting picture possible of their otherwise pathetic existence.

IN: But that's not it entirely.

CB: No. Even when I've seen myself, I feel like a disconnected observer. It's me, but it's also not me that I am watching.

IN: Who is it?

CB: Some other Casey. Future Casey.

IN: But it is you.

CB: Obviously.

IN: As long as you are aware of that.

CB: I guess what I'm trying to say is that it doesn't feel like it's me. And if I were to tell you what I see down the road for myself, it would probably sound a lot like the recordings you claim to have enjoyed hearing.

IN: Are you addicted to seeing?

CB: I don't think so.

IN: Since you brought up seeing yourself, do you think we could talk about what you saw that first time you did a reading on yourself? Or is that still a no-go?

CB: Sure, I'm up for it.

IN: Why the change of heart?

CB: You're growing on me, [redacted].

IN: I—

CB: In a friendly way, I'm not here to hit on you.

IN: I feel compelled to remind you that I am not your friend.

CB: That's okay, all that matters is if I like you.

IN: And why is that?

CB: Do you want to hear what I saw when I read for myself, or not?

IN: Please, go ahead.

CB: I saw a day where I could no longer read.

IN: And that was a bad thing?

CB: Well, to be more specific, I saw a day where my inability to read enraged David. He was convinced that I still could. So certain, in fact, that in order to make me continue reading for him, he was willing to torture a woman and her family, directly in front of me, to jog my ability.

IN: That's awful, I'm sorry. This was Lylian I assume?

CB: Does it matter what woman it was, really?

IN: No. I suppose it shouldn't.

CB: It wasn't one of his people. Let's just leave it at that.

IN: And this is when you decided to leave David's?

CB: Escaping had always been on the backburner of my mind. When I came out of that vision, I decided we would try to make a run for it the very next day.

IN: How did the two of you actually do that?

CB: It wasn't uncommon for me to run around the property, which was hundreds of scrubby acres.

IN: They weren't watching you?

CB: They had been, for sure, at least at first. Men perched on the roof at all times. And any time I ran, I heard small drones zipping about above me. I ran a lot, all over, and I always returned. I think over time his men assumed my obedience would be a forever thing.

IN: Lylian though?

CB: It wasn't unusual for her to join me. She'd been out with me on foot or a mountain bike enough times to make it seem equally common.

IN: The day you did escape, had you told Lylian that was the plan?

CB: No.

IN: Why not?

CB: Seemed safer.

IN: You didn't trust her?

CB: Not entirely. She was seeing Ruby regularly. We were under David's thumb, sure, but he was hardly ever around. We wanted for nothing, but more than that, I think she truly believed a day would come where David would decide her debt had been paid.

IN: But you'd already seen otherwise?

CB: In some sense, yeah.

IN: She never mentioned escaping?

CB: No. I only heard her thoughts on the matter after the fact.

IN: Which were?

CB: I'd kill myself for Lylian, and I believe she loves me, but—

IN: She was willing to stay at David's forever to protect Ruby.

CB: It's understandable. Not easy to accept, but understandable.

IN: She was angry, then?

CB: She was resigned to our new freedom. It wasn't that she hadn't daydreamed about a life outside the compound, but she was justifiably focused on Ruby's welfare.

IN: And so, how did you manage to exit? What about the drones?

CB: I wasn't hearing the drones as often. And the men on the roof were spending more time on their phones than on watching me. Or watching us for that matter.

IN: David's people got sloppy, or maybe believed you were suffering from Stockholm Syndrome?

CB: Maybe. All I know is when we set out that afternoon, no one suspected shit. Not even Lyl. I'd run along the property's edge countless times. We left the house and headed west. Later in the day. I had never been up on the roof, but I imagined the light from that direction was blinding around that time. We reached the cattle wire and simply climbed through. Nothing to it. I went first, told Lylian to hand me the bike, and then she came over and off we went.

IN: Lylian just went along willingly, no questions asked?

CB: Well, yes and no. There is a magic to a moment like that. At least there was for me. I assumed she was all-in, that the action itself had put her own survival instincts in gear. She was quiet, compliant for lack of a better word. We raced in one direction until dark, got lucky and found a forgotten barn to hide in overnight. I'll admit, the whole thing was far easier than I had expected it to be, our escape *and* Lylian's cooperation.

IN: Is it possible she thought you were going to get caught?

CB: Exactly! She thought if she was with me when I got caught, David's punishment would be less severe.

IN: But you didn't get caught. That must have been surprising.

CB: Yes, I was surprised. I hadn't planned much beyond our leaving David's property and making an ill-advised run for it. We stayed off the main road, there were no SUVs bearing down on us, no choppers, no drones, no nothing. There is a lot of land to cover in that part of Texas, so I figured we had gotten obscenely lucky.

IN: What happened the next day?

CB: We found the keys to a truck, inside the truck, outside of a trailer home that showed very few signs of recent inhabitation. Neither of us believed we would somehow make it to Arizona before David—I mean, he knew where Ruby was staying—but somehow, we did.

IN: You went there straight away.

CB: I get the sense you have heard this story already.

IN: You've told me this story before, Casey.

4

He is stirring.

Casey is sandwiched between the whisper-quiet hum of two turbofan engines, his body shifting in its oversized recliner.

Just a few feet in front of him, Cooper is wide awake, staring into the dark heavens that lurk on the other side of the jet's oval window. He is unaware of Casey's revival, or indifferent to it.

The pace of Casey's twitches and quivers quickens. His senses are awakening. He is up, then out. Up, then out. Struggling between incoherent and jumbled bearings. When it seems he might go straight back down, Casey shakes himself free, a fog about him.

His hands are bound, tucked between his back and the chair. He can pivot a bit from where his torso meets his hips, but not much else. He rocks left and right on his buttocks, blinks himself into lucidity.

"Ah, you're awake," Cooper says happily. "Finally, a little company. Everyone else is O-U-T."

Cooper's declaration kicks Casey over the finish line. He is now, by definition, awake.

Cooper leans forward in a clumsy attempt to brush the

frayed curtain of dark hair away from Casey's eyes. He pushes it to one side and then to the other. Neither direction sticks and he shrugs as if to say *I tried* as he finds his own comfort again.

"How was the nap?" he asks. "You should thank me for sedating you. You looked like utter dog shit last night." He pushes his thick body deeper into his seat. "You still look like dog shit, actually."

"I appreciate your concern," Casey says. His focus roams. He tries to collate the details of his surroundings.

On the other side of the tiny aisle to his left, Lylian is similarly bound and out cold. Like Casey, her clothes have been changed. Beneath a sheer blouse, her chest rises and falls to an unnaturally slow tempo. It carries a black obsidian pendant, up and down, with the wait-and-see steadiness of a metronome on its very lowest setting.

Casey bought her the necklace as a lark weeks before she murdered Diego. According to the shop clerk, the stone is rumored to block psychic attacks. At a minimum, it's supposed to absorb negative energy. It was performing about as well as he had expected it to.

Cooper puts a heavy grip on Casey's shoulder and yanks him away from Lylian's direction.

"She could use the sleep, don't you think? You've put her through a lot."

Casey bites his lip, begrudgingly agrees, "sure," then leans back into his seat. He fights to hide his shivers while still evaluating Lylian.

"Can you get her a blanket at least? It's fucking freezing in here."

Cooper makes a sardonic wave in front of the vents blowing over their heads. He rolls his hand back and forth in the air.

"It's gotta be seventy-eight degrees in here, Casey. Might be time to put some meat between your bones and your skin, don't you think?"

"Come on, man. Just give her your blanket."

Cooper sighs, then grabs the tightly rolled travel linen resting on the wooden shelf between his armrest and the fuselage's quilted fabric interior. He stands to unfurl it, then shakes the cashmere rectangle to form and gently places it over her. It only covers her from neck to knees. She remains unmoved.

Cooper senses Casey's anxiety, stands, then reaches behind him, releasing his arms from their restraints.

"See?" Cooper says with his stomach still pressed into Casey's face. "I'm reasonable enough for the three of us." He takes a step back. "Go on, go see your girl."

Casey works quick to unbuckle his lap belt, then moves across the aisle as Cooper sits back down.

"I'm guessing I don't have to tell you there's nowhere to run on this thing," Cooper adds.

Casey hovers over Lylian. He drops to his knees, then puts two hideous fingers to the pulse on her neck. He lets his hand rest on her chest next, up and down with the swell of her breathing. The two vitals do little to remove his concern. He contorts the blanket in a way that might cover more of her, but there is no give to the fabric and no direction to the covering that makes a significant difference. Casey lays his head upon her lap, her body remains motionless.

"It's possible the guys gave her an amount that's more than someone her size requires," Cooper admits. He might actually be sorry, at least he sounds like he's sorry. "She'll be fine though, I promise."

Casey stands to return to his seat. The backs of two large heads poke over their rests, closer to the cockpit.

"Friends of yours?" Casey asks, pointing at them.

"We're all friends here. At least as far as I'm concerned."

Casey nods unwittingly while returning his attention to Lylian. He sits, but there is no peace in the act.

They are both silent for a while, with only an ear on the purr of the engines.

Casey explores the various nicks, dents, and swellings of his body. He picks and prods at each, starting at his wrists, then moving up his arms until he finishes the job at his forehead. The mild disgust on Cooper's face brings Casey's search party to a halt. He forces his hands to his lap, interlaces his fingers with determined intent, then tries to shake Cooper from his loathing with a kindergartener's practiced smile.

"When was the last time you took a good look at yourself in the mirror?" Cooper asks.

"It's been a while."

Cooper wasn't expecting an actual answer.

"A long time for someone like me, anyway."

Casey's eyes land at the jet's lavatory door, a deep stare on it that is uncomfortably long. His desire is obvious.

"Go for it," Cooper says. "We've got plenty of time before we touch down."

Casey just barely lifts himself from his seat, pauses, then sits back down.

Cooper is indifferent. "Suit yourself," he shrugs. "The way you look right now? Probably for the best."

The barb isn't that sharp, but it has a noticeable effect.

"I doubt some shit piece of plastic, coated in cheap tin, hanging over an outhouse at forty-five thousand feet is worth the effort," Casey says.

Cooper laughs.

"It wasn't a joke, dumbfuck."

Cooper quiets quick.

"You don't have to like me, Casey. Hell, I can't say I much care for you. But when all is said and done, I promise: you, your girl, and Ruby, all get to head off into some sunset somewhere in one piece."

He's uncomfortable with his attempt at kindness, unable to sit with it, and he peppers the promise with another gibe.

"Shit. Maybe you have already *seen* me do that for you."

Casey doesn't respond. He has returned his attention to Lylian, and he doesn't leave the monotony of her medulla's work as he probes Cooper for details.

"I assume your plan is a bit different now."

"Well, they didn't have Ruby before," Cooper says, "now did they?"

"Any chance we can leave Lylian out of the new plan?" Casey asks.

Cooper laughs again, harder than he needs to this time. It is a bellicose roar that does its best to add more shake to the already vibrating cabin, yet not enough to awaken Lylian or the two sagging heads up front.

"I'll admit, I don't know your gal all that well. But she hardly seems like the type to take a backseat. Her ex has their little girl again. All to himself. She's not gonna sit this out."

Casey takes a deep breath, the kind that precede preposterous truths.

"David doesn't want Lylian, Cooper. He wants me."

It is subtle, but there's a transient crack in Cooper's always in-charge façade. He seals the fissure quickly. Fakes it to make it behind the steely grin that sits so well under dark brown eyes and a well-lived nose. True or not, Casey's assertion keeps Cooper's attention away from Lylian's sprouting activity. It is the tiniest buds of motion. Her zygomaticus major and minor muscles tense covertly under her flushed cheeks.

"You should let me read for you," Casey says. The urgency in his suggestion is patent.

Cooper dismisses the idea with a huff before turning to look out his window again.

"I'm serious, Cooper. What have you got to lose? Let me look into your future."

Cooper doesn't budge, doesn't leave the dark sky outside.

"If you're hungry, Casey, just walk yourself upfront there and grab some fuckin' peanuts."

"Hear me out," Casey says. "Let me look ahead and see if your plan is a success." He brings his hands to either armrest and balls them up. If there is going to be punching, he may as well present as an expectant punching bag. "I'm sure all I'll report back is that it's going to work out brilliantly. But, on the off chance that your plan sucks, wouldn't it be better to know now instead of after?"

Cooper shakes his head, then returns to the unspeaking sky outside. He shows no bend in his disbelief.

"I wouldn't believe you... even if I letcha."

There is some waffle in his voice.

"Let's make you a believer," Casey pounces. "How long until we land?"

Cooper brings the military grade watch on his wrist to his face. He takes a longer than needed look.

"Another couple of hours, Chief."

"That is plenty of time for me to read for you."

"I'm not lookin' to see what awaits us when we get to Texas, Casey."

His attempt to shut Casey down sounds half-hearted.

"I'm talking about your more immediate future, the one that will happen right here on this plane, before we land."

Cooper swivels away from the window, leans over his shoes and puts his face square to Casey's. He clicks his tongue, clicks it again. Casey's fists are frozen. His body tenses, resigns to taking the brunt. Cooper rolls his head on his neck, stretches his way into considering the idea.

"Okay, asshole. I'm as bored as anyone. I'll play. Whaddya got in mind?"

"Alright... great," Casey says, hardly able to contain his shock at breaking Cooper down. He scrambles to assemble next-steps before he loses Cooper's interest. "In about an hour, I want you to leave me here. Go sit upfront with your friends and just talk to them—"

"About what?"

"About anything," Casey says. "So long as it is detailed, very specific. Something you think I would never be able to guess you were talking about with them."

"I don't follow."

"It's simple: I'll go to the galley, grab what snacks I can, then shovel it down. I'm sure there's enough to jump onto your timeline, roughly one hour from now, right here on this plane. That's not far ahead, it won't take much food or much time. If I have a vision, I won't tell you what I've seen until *after* you have finished your chat. I'll keep it a secret. Then, you go up there, say anything you want, and when you come back, I should be able to tell you exactly what happened and what you said. In detail."

Adrenaline has given Casey a second wind. He doesn't wait for Cooper to agree, stands quickly and turns toward the kitchen.

"And then what?" Cooper asks as he throws his leg in front of Casey, stopping his momentum.

"If what I say I saw and what you know you just did match, there's your proof that I'm not bullshitting you when I say I can see the future. Then, after we land, you let me read for you again. If in my vision I see that your plan to snag David fails, we spitball something new. Something using only me. A plan that doesn't put Lylian in any more danger."

"And if you're wrong?" Cooper asks.

"Name it. Whatever you want."

The big moose pinches his nostrils deliberately, hanging on to them as he conjures up a contribution to the wager. He takes his time, looking away just to keep Casey agog. You can almost see the lightbulb go on over his head when he arrives at a prize he considers worth betting over.

"If you're wrong, we race when there's time. After David, after all of this. Ten miles. Both of us rested, and after you've had a chance to get into better shape."

"You want to *race* me? That's your half of the bet?"

"I want to race you fairly. A healthy you versus a healthy me."

Casey doesn't hesitate. "You got it."

Cooper sinks confidently into his chair. His body relaxes in the certain belief he's just made a bet that he won't lose. "Okay then," he says with an upbeat grin, "what do I do now?"

"You sit, I eat. You can watch me eat if you want," Casey says midway to the galley. "It's up to you."

He walks past Cooper's men and they don't budge. Both are wearing blackout sleep masks, headphones pushed deep into their oversized ears. The racket made by Casey's frantic effort to raid the pantry, fridge, and countertop doesn't draw them out of their slumber. There are plenty of snacks to choose from. Casey hones in on sustenance that is both quick to consume and has a calories per serving count of over one hundred. Not all of it will be easy to cookie-toss later, but he could do worse.

"You want me to eat all this up here? It's not for the faint—"

"No, no. Bring it all here," Cooper crows. "I'm curious."

Casey grabs the bottom of his shirt in one hand and pulls the hem out in front of himself to fashion a fabric basket. In it he carries ten single-serve bleu cheese dressings, ten single-serve Caesar dressings, a half-dozen premium mayonnaise packets, six croissants, six cinnamon raisin bagels, and two bottles of small-batch cola. The bounty bounds in front of him as he heads back to their seats.

Casey motions for Cooper to bring out the pocketed table from the wall. He sets out the spread of edibles between them.

Lylian's posture has noticeably shifted. Casey pauses the chaos, says her name just to be sure she hasn't come to. She doesn't respond. He pulls off the colored foil from the first condiment's tiny plastic drum.

"This won't be the ugliest meal I've ever used, Cooper, but are you sure you want to watch me put all this down?" He doesn't wait for an answer as he turns the cup's rim to his mouth.

"Knock yourself out, Casey."

Three cups of Bleu Cheese into the reading, Cooper alters the bet.

"One thing," he says, and motions to the scattered mini-feast on the table, "there's absolutely no throwing up all of these *snacks* when you are done. Not aboard this aluminum kite."

Casey looks to the lavatory as he sucks all the mayo out of its packet.

"Not even in there," Cooper says. "I'll smell it no matter where you do it. And I'm not havin' it, got it? Eat, read, and keep that shit in your stomach where it belongs."

Casey's mouth is too full to protest. It's working around half a bagel coated in Caesar dressing. He looks to Lylian, then turns back to Cooper and reluctantly nods.

"Atta boy, then. Get after it."

Subject: CASEY BANKS
Interviewer: [redacted]
Date of Interview: 11/25/2015
CB=Casey Banks, IN=Interviewer

IN: This interview is being recorded. The time is 11:11AM. How are you feeling this morning, Casey?

CB: Bloated. Uncomfortable. Huge.

IN: Did you force yourself to vomit at the end of yesterday's reading?

CB: I did. I am not looking for sympathy. Not trying to evade this interview either.

IN: Are you vomiting during the off weeks in between reading weeks?

CB: I don't read during off weeks.

IN: Good to hear, but that's not what I asked.

CB: I plead the fifth.

IN: I'm sure your discomfort is real. Physically, mentally. One week off here and there is not enough time for any significant recovery.

CB: I'm aware.

IN: Your gastrointestinal tract needs time to heal. There's more than a handful of reasons you are distended. But you aren't gaining weight, I can assure you. Weakened muscles, compromised digestive enzymes, your gut's bacteria are probably non-existent. At this point, even the small amount you allow yourself to eat during a down-week day is going to be a living hell on your digestive system. At least for a while. That's doubly true if you are evacuating those tiny meals as well.

CB: [redacted], you asked me how I felt, I told you. I wasn't looking for you to outline a cure.

IN: There is a point of no return here, you know.

CB: Death is an inevitability for us all.

IN: Are you having suicidal thoughts?

CB: No.

IN: If you were, would you tell me?

CB: I believe I would, yes.

IN: A premature death is just one possibility. Your disorders, even when tacked to a schedule meant to minimize them, will ultimately lead to some very nasty, long-term effects—if not life-long.

CB: I've told you before, I don't plan on doing this forever.

IN: I hear that a lot from my patients.

CB: Are any of them also able to see the future?

IN: This isn't the first time you've said that you believed there was an end to all this. You believe that or you've seen that?

CB: How will the world know me? I know what I want to be. Who I want to be for Lylian and Ruby. Who I can be, in the service of a better life for the both of them. For us all.

IN: How will the world know you?

CB: My father.

IN: William.

CB: A William-ism, yes.

IN: Can we come back to your father in this session?

CB: Where are we headed now?

IN: How are you feeling about continuing to perform readings with us?

CB: I'm game to keep at it if the team believes it will lead to some answers.

IN: What are you hoping to hear?

CB: I want to know why I can see. I want an explanation.

IN: If they ever arrive at a solid conclusion, what would you do with that information?

CB: I don't know. I just want an answer to 'why me?'

IN: Do you believe that you are alone in seeing?

CB: Are there others? Fuck me, of course there are. How fucking obvious. You must think I'm a real self-centered dipshit.

IN: I don't—

CB: I'm not the only person with this ability, right? There are other subjects here?

IN: Subjects, yes.

CB: Well, fuck me twice then.

IN: You are upset.

CB: No. I'm just embarrassed that, until now, it had not occurred to me that you would be taking what you learn about me and trying to replicate the power with other people.

IN: You shouldn't be embarrassed. We've kept you pretty busy.

CB: I'm a fucking how-to video.

IN: I think you are diminishing the importance of the research itself.

CB: So?

IN: I'm sorry, so what?

CB: Are the other subjects seeing?

IN: (inaudible)

CB: Don't look for permission on the other side of that mirror, just fucking tell me or we walk. Today.

IN: No other seers, yet, I'm afraid.

CB: I'm not sure if I should be happy or sad about that.

IN: Locating willing participants, who've adhered to a lifestyle similar to yours, and have done so for as long as you have, has been difficult.

CB: Calling all anorexics, help us prove that eating a shit-ton of food might just let you see the future! I can see how that might be a bitch of an experiment to seat.

IN: Not exactly how we worded it, but yes.

CB: Fucking hell, I feel dumb.

IN: I am sorry. Obviously, you are not.

CB: You should be paying me to be here.

IN: We've housed you, fed you. This organization is likely the only reason Ruby and Marion are safe and sound.

CB: It was a bad joke. Jesus. Who isn't taking credit for Ruby's safety these days? You, Cooper, David. Let me tell you something, Ruby is going to be just fine and it sure as shit isn't going to have anything to do with this outfit.

IN: That's good to hear.

CB: You will let me know if something changes though, right?

With one of the other subjects?

IN: That's not my call to make.

CB: Got it. Honestly, I'm not sure if I care.

IN: I want to remind you that being here is your decision. Nobody benefits from forced observation.

CB: Does Lylian want to leave?

IN: Have you asked her yourself?

CB: She didn't want to leave David's. She may not want to bounce from this situation either. Your people have eyes on Ruby and Lylian's mother, or did I just hallucinate that detail? If I was her, I'd probably rank your ability to keep Ruby safe high above my own.

IN: The safety of anyone you care about is paramount to us, to our research, and to the desired outcome. I can't speak for Lylian, but I do think you should discuss your feelings about leaving with her.

CB: When did I last see Lylian?

IN: You can't recall on your own?

CB: I saw her yesterday.

IN: Your recent short-term memory lapses are troubling. For the past two weeks you have been showing symptoms of imbalances in certain serotonin receptor activity. Memory, attention span, motivation, concentration, any and all of these things can be seriously impacted by the habitual practice of eating disorders. I'd like to ask you to postpone any additional readings until there is marked improvement.

CB: You are going to stop the readings?

IN: No. I'm asking you to stop them. Temporarily. It's your decision and yours alone.

CB: I don't buy that.

IN: Casey, I can't continue, the group can't continue, if you don't absolutely accept that you are in total control of your situation here.

CB: I am in control of my situation.

IN: Total control.

CB: Total control.

IN: That's a start.

CB: I'll consider a longer pause in between readings.

IN: Thank you. I'll advise the team of that.

CB: So, you wanted to talk about my father?

IN: William, yes.

CB: He is hardly relevant to any of this.

IN: You killed him when you were ten.

CB: I shot him. Accidentally.

IN: Patricide is consequential, even if accidental.

CB: Taking a ten-year-old quail hunting in August in East Texas isn't without risk.

IN: (inaudible)

CB: May as well call it regicide.

IN: The killing of kings?

CB: To many powerful men, he was one.

IN: Were you aware of his standing? As a child?

CB: He helmed an all-male congregation, titans of what passed as innovation at the time. A bunch of old, white, fat fucks plunked about pleather, reveling in the excess they believed they had earned. The back room at the Piedmont was the closest thing to a castle I had seen before age ten. So yes, William seemed like a king to me.

IN: My loose understanding is that, once a year, William invited many of the wealthiest business owners in Texas to come to your hometown for something billed as a rich man's brainstorming.

CB: Sure. You could call it that, but don't forget the hookers.

IN: You sound disapproving of the event?

CB: His motivation was alright.

IN: Which was?

CB: Solutions. Big solutions for big problems. Not just the obstacles facing the wealthy, but those of the everyman.

IN: That's respectable—

CB: Booze-fueled idea exchanges with his "peers." Infinite monkey theorem with hairless apes and no typewriters. His guests had money, but money doesn't buy smarts, not like my father's. And, more often than not, making obscene amounts of money destroys one's capacity for empathy.

IN: Did any significant ideas come from any get-together?

CB: Of course, they did.

IN: Like what?

CB: It's not like they invented the umbrella.

IN: So, what were they responsible for?

CB: Unless you're ready for a deep dive into how safety improvements to hydrocrackers helped save lives, or what role big oil might have played in DNA fingerprinting, can I just skip to the point?

IN: I'm intrigued by both, but go ahead.

CB: He didn't care who took the credit, trademarked or patented them, so long as the ideas themselves were realized. I suppose that's noble. He understood their motivations too, and if that meant staging out-of-town hookers as chain-smoking, local barflies at The Piedmont's bar, so be it. Whatever landed funding.

IN: How did Virginia Anne feel about these events?

CB: Mom knew who she married.

IN: And the town?

CB: They fucking loved him for it. Spring, Texas had no legitimate claim to anything worth memorializing or advertising. Dad's conferences were the closest thing we had to a tourist attraction. Local businesses gouged, taps ran dry, The Piedmont collecting something like sixty percent of its annual revenue in just those three or four days alone. Had my father asked the local law to temporarily allow casual murder, they might have considered it. If that is not a king, I don't know what one is.

IN: It seems like you have a lot of respect for your father.

CB: It is possible to carry both respect and contempt for a man, and easier when he is blood.

IN: But you don't see any connection between your relationship with him and your life now.

CB: I didn't say that.

IN: So, your anorexia, your seeing, you do see a connection, then?

CB: Right, my anorexia. Look, I was the child they made, and now I am the adult they helped shape. I don't have to be an expert in genealogy or sociology to understand how pivotal

William and my mother were in fashioning the mess before you. But, connected to seeing? That is not my diagnosis to make.

IN: How would you classify their parenting style?

CB: I don't think it *has* been classified.

IN: If you had to classify it, could you?

CB: Are you familiar with Infantile Omnipotence?

IN: I believe it's the term used to describe the exaggerated sense of self-importance in infants.

CB: Exactly. Center of the universe, every need addressed, every whim entertained. Left unchecked, as a child ages, he believes himself to be all-powerful and that the rest of humanity exists to serve him.

IN: Freud?

CB: Bingo. I'd say William developed his own approach to child-rearing, loosely based on Infantile Omnipotence.

IN: Do you think of yourself as a narcissist?

CB: How will the world know you? Does it get any more narcissistic than that? It's all about what am I presenting to the world. Not necessarily who you are actually.

IN: I'm not sure I'd have interpreted the question that way.

CB: The age you are asked the question might come into play.

IN: How old were you when he asked it?

CB: I'm certain he asked it from day one. I trust my memory, but I understand it to be a complex mechanism. By my recollection, not a day went by during my adolescence that he didn't put the question to me.

IN: Did you have an answer?

CB: Early on, I'm sure I said Fireman, Construction Worker, Doctor, the usual. As I got older, I came to feel the answer he was looking for was something along the lines of 'a very decent man.'

IN: And why is that?

CB: Maybe because that's what he wanted me to believe he was... a very decent man.

IN: Wasn't he?

CB: There is no one binding definition.

IN: Sounds like you have some doubts.

CB: I was born a few months after one of William's events went sideways. There was a gang rape. A local woman that was not one of the prostitutes on my dad's payroll. The town was worried the assault would mean the end of their yearly boon, but my father negotiated a settlement with the victim. She was a good friend of his, and it handled it personally. She left Spring and the townsfolk moved on like nothing had ever happened.

IN: And what about the men who committed the assault?

CB: No one was charged with anything.

IN: I'm sorry to say that's all-too typical.

CB: That's not entirely true—

IN: I beg to differ.

CB: The town moving on, I mean. Come to think of it, they speculated a lot on her, gossiped about her whereabouts, and whether she'd kept the baby or not. Whether it was a boy or girl. Who of the men was actually the father—

IN: She was pregnant?

CB: Apparently.

5

He sits alone in makeshift ignorance.

The darkness that shrouds Casey is one he agreed to.

A black hood covers his head. His arms are bound tight behind his back again. Cooper's cheap, noise-cancelling headphones are pumping tunes into Casey's ears at several decibels above what is necessary to hide the conversation Cooper agreed to have.

He looks every bit the violent terrorist. All that remains of the meal Casey consumed is an unopened soda and half a bagel. The fervent spectacle of workmanlike scarfing has given way to a patient and motionless pose of wait-and-see.

Lylian is still out, also cloaked, in a less impromptu fashion.

For all I know, you two are in cahoots, Cooper'd said.

Her eyes are hidden behind a satin sleep mask, her ears stuffed with light blue foam earplugs.

Three rows closer to the cockpit, Cooper matches the motion of the bird's indecision, his bulk towering haphazardly over the sleeping heads of his two-man team. He left Lylian and Casey at their seats ten minutes ago, but hasn't committed to any action. He stares at the back of Casey's stillness, has been for some time.

There is a quick hit of routine turbulence. The bobble jars Cooper's focus. "Just have a conversation… use specific words… then I'll tell you what you did," he mumbles in a voice meant to mimic Casey barking his instructions earlier. "Fine then, here goes nothing."

Cooper takes the recliner across from Jim, then leans forward and shakes his soldier from sleep. The commotion wakes the second solid mass sitting at Cooper's right, that man instinctively grabs for the Glock 9-millimeter resting in his shoulder holster. Cooper's hand puts a lightning-quick stop to the misunderstanding, deescalates the situation before Jim has even pulled the sleep-aid away from his eyes.

"Jesus, Cooper. I thought you said we could grab a few."

Both men are instantly wide-awake with an immediate energy honed for survival. Their faces soften with a light resentment that Cooper blithely ignores by quickly talking into their irritation.

"Sorry, Daryl. I did say that. This won't take that long."

"What's up, then?" Jim asks.

Cooper's attention goes back toward Casey, who is exactly as he'd left him: hood over his head, hands bound, entirely immobile and with thumping bass blasting into his ears. Lylian hasn't moved.

"Are we talking about something here?" Daryl asks.

Cooper ignores their growing impatience. He investigates the air around them, looking to his left, then his right, then above. It's as if he hopes to see some evidential remnant of Casey from the past, now snooping around the four-seat cluster to observe them.

"I wouldn't mind trying to crawl right back into the dream I just left," Daryl adds.

Cooper is tongue-tied.

"What dream was that?" Jim asks suggestively.

"You'd like to know, you fuckin' homo."

Cooper breaks from his momentary inertia.

"Keep your voices down," he says.

He is clearly struggling to come up with a topic to talk about. His wheels not so much turning as grinding to a near halt.

"Sorry," Cooper finally commits, "I just don't get it."

"Get what?" Jim asks.

"You know... them two," he says, motioning a hand in the direction of Lylian and Casey. "It just doesn't add up."

Neither man makes any effort to turn his head.

"C'mon, Cooper," says Jim. "It's not like this is the first time we've seen some hot snatch stuck to the hip of an ugly mother-fucker. Probably got a great personality. Why, you got a soft spot for her?"

Cooper grimaces and shifts his lower anatomy.

"Hell, if you don't, I might have a go," Daryl says, turning to take a long peer at Lylian. "I see you threw a mask on her, that was awful sweet of you."

Cooper's heavy right fist races from his thigh and into Daryl's pec, then returns to his lap with a speed that should impress them all. But it doesn't. Neither's body stiffened during the assault and the two men remain un-wooed.

"Dumbass," Jim says, shaking his head.

"Do you think she's actually into him?" Cooper asks. "Or just using him?"

The question is awkward. His grade-school approach is absolutely painful to watch. For a moment, the man looks every bit like a boy.

Daryl and Jim work hard to kill growing smirks.

"Using him?" Jim manages to ask.

"Using him for what?" Daryl adds.

They hang in a state of wonder only Cooper can resolve, but he's stuck in a hesitancy he's had since the chat's start.

"He's loaded, of course," Cooper says. "Some time ago, that scrawny little fuck became the heir to a massive fuckin' fortune."

"How much we talkin' about?" Jim asks. His curiosity is legitimate now.

"Enough," Cooper says. "That's all you two need to know."

"Some faggots have all the luck," Daryl says.

Cooper's muscles tighten. A physical rebuke might be imminent, but Cooper caves, sinks deeper into the embrace of his chair.

Jim has a squirm about him. Like Daryl, he has his sleep mask back on his lap, rubs it impatiently between his thumb and finger. Cooper is indifferent to the hint. He stretches his neck to look over and past the two men, his eyes refusing to leave the back of Casey's head.

"Well, fuck, man. If this guy's also got money, maybe we're looking at two big payouts when we take care of David," Daryl says.

Cooper's face twists. It's obvious he hadn't expected Daryl to reveal so much. His general ambivalence to their conversation evaporates. He breathes deeply, and the inhalation projects his intense displeasure. Daryl and Jim shrink into the posture of children who are intimately familiar with the signs of impending punishment.

"Yeah, maybe," Cooper surprises them.

He pushes himself up from his seat.

"Sleep again if you can. Honestly, I'm sorry I woke you both. Just bored I guess."

As he heads to the back, his men exchange wide eyes.

"What the fuck was that?" Daryl whispers quietly, but Jim has already put the sleep mask back on his face.

Casey's body lifts a little as it senses Cooper approaching. The engines growl and whirr in descent as Cooper rubs his face deep with one hand. He reaches behind Casey and removes the bindings, then plucks the black hood from his head. Casey removes the headphones and holds them out for Cooper to take.

"Keep 'em."

Cooper drops into his seat and his face is stone. It's as if he believes saying anything, or even allowing an expression, will tip-off Casey, give him some clue to the conversation he's just had—a conversation that Casey is supposed to know in full-detail.

The various mechanisms caterwaul along the aircraft's underbelly and Lylian comes out of her stupor. She is far from fully awake, but Casey's moment is dwindling.

"Did you really think you'd see me hanging around, spying on you three? I'm not some two-bit time traveller."

Cooper's cheeks burn. "Fuck off. You said specifics, so, let's hear some details."

"How did you know about my inheritance?" Casey asks.

"I work for the government. Do the math. Is that all you've got?"

"Isn't that detail enough?"

"Hardly."

"It's not my money, you know. Not mine to spend anyway," Casey says.

"I don't think that's how family endowments work, but—"

"Look," Casey interrupts, "I'm not saying that Lylian isn't using me as you suggested up there. For fuck's sake, she had me working for David. She was quite literally using me to keep her and Ruby safe. But I can tell you for sure, she doesn't know about that money."

"Two for two, keep going," Cooper eggs him on.

"Okay. I'm thinking Daryl is more than a little homophobic. You spent most of the conversation just looking at the back of my head. Jim called me an ugly motherfucker. At one point, they figured you might have a thing for Lyl, and, given the chance, Daryl made it pretty clear he would try to fuck Lylian. Should I go on?"

"No. That'll do."

Cooper grabs for the unopened cola, twists off the top, and after a long sip, continues, "I'll admit, it's a nifty trick, Casey. Disgusting as hell to watch a man eat like that, but nifty nonetheless."

Lylian's arms fight to come out from behind her body. She drops her temple into her shoulder to inch the mask off her face.

The plane's wheels find the ground with a quick bounce and pop. The engines reverse to drop speed.

"So, you believe me," Casey hurries.

"Sure, I believe you."

"And you'll give me another chance to read?" he asks. "To see if what you've planned actually pans out?"

"Nope, she's still the plan," Cooper says, pointing at Lylian. "None of this hocus-pocus has changed my mind... Not about using her anyway."

With one eye on Lylian's improving composure, Casey drops his volume to a fierce whisper.

"Fuck you, Cooper, and fuck whoever is paying you to go after David. Fuck you both, whoever you actually are."

Cooper throws a full fist, but just like a cartoon, he manages to stop its brute force a hair's width away from Casey's face.

"I'm exactly who I told you I am." He pulls his fist back to his lap. "Just a guy trying to help you three to a happier ending."

Casey puts a hand to his stomach, remembers the meal. He goes green as he surveys the landscape of discarded wrappers, packets, and containers on the table. He looks at the lavatory door.

"I'm going to go make myself throw up," he says. "You owe me that."

He stands, but Cooper kicks him hard back into his chair.

"No fucking way. I don't owe you shit," Cooper says.

Casey's throat subtly balloons. From there, the convulsion inflates his cheeks.

"Don't you do it," Cooper demands.

There's a gurgle, he's close.

"I'm deadly serious, Casey, try me. Swallow your mistake."

Casey holds out for as long as he can, then forces the upchuck back, adding his own sound effect to punctuate his obedience.

"Now try and learn from it," Cooper says. "God knows I am."

Subject: CASEY BANKS
Interviewer: [redacted]
Date of Interview: 12/11/2015
CB=Casey Banks, IN=Interviewer

IN: This interview is being recorded. The time is—

CB: Where in the hell have you been, [redacted]?

IN: It was Thanksgiving.

CB: Thanksgiving was fifteen days ago.

IN: For some people, Christmas is the big holiday. For my family, it's Thanksgiving. The whole bunch takes time off around then.

CB: Bullshit.

IN: I have pictures, would you like to see them?

CB: Where did you go?

IN: This year it was Hawaii. Last year it was Vancouver. The year before that, my family and my husband's family all made the journey to Australia, should I go on?

CB: Why didn't you tell me you would be gone?

IN: I apologize. In hindsight, I should have. Would it have mattered?

CB: Maybe.

IN: I was happy to find out you were still here. And a bit surprised, to be honest. The team has informed me that you are on the backend of an extended break from readings, that—

CB: You thought we'd leave?

IN: I thought you and Lylian might go, yes.

CB: What gave you that impression?

IN: Before my break, your commitment seemed shaky. And, statistically, people in your situation tend to come and go a few times before the real progress begins.

CB: Progress with what? Reading?

IN: I'm talking about your eating disorders, of course.

CB: Am I in rehab?

IN: No. Not exactly. I don't think there's a recovery center on earth that would condone binging and purging as part of any qualified program. Even if it was to see the future or happening under observation. Still, I have high hopes for you.

CB: I don't understand.

IN: You are here to read. The other members of the team are here because they want to know why it is you can do that. It is also true that, personally, I would like to see a healthier version of Casey Banks leave this facility. I suppose it's just my nature.

CB: You want me to stop reading altogether?

IN: I believe in baby steps.

CB: What then?

IN: Well, for starters, I'd be happy if you gave up the bulimic part of your journey. Have you?

CB: I haven't read since just before our last conversation.

IN: Your evasions aren't helpful.

CB: I haven't thrown-up since after that reading.

IN: That's wonderful. I'm really glad to hear it. I don't mind telling you it shows.

CB: Are you saying I'm fat?

IN: I'm saying you look well. At least for a guy who I assume didn't actually eat much in the weeks I was gone.

CB: 'Well' is a vague adjective.

IN: What's an adjective that I could use that you *would* believe, Casey?

CB: (inaudible)

IN: What was that?

CB: I said, why are you a part of this?

IN: I think they've hired me because of my experience.

CB: Which is?

IN: Eating disorders. I would have thought that that was abundantly clear by now.

CB: But what is in it for you? Beyond helping people.

IN: Are you asking if I am being paid?

CB: Not exactly. For all I know, you are being forced to perform your role.

IN: By whom?

CB: How would I know?

IN: Funny.

CB: So... you are just in it for the money.

IN: I'll admit, when the team approached me, I didn't believe your story. When they told me what they were willing to pay me to be a part of this research, I decided it didn't matter if I believed your story. It is possible to want to help while also wanting to be paid.

CB: Am I the only rat in this lab not getting paid?

IN: I couldn't say.

CB: If I were to leave today, would the team terminate your contract?

IN: Probably. I suppose they might reach out to me if they had any additional questions, but I'm not banking on that.

CB: I stay, you keep getting paid. Don't you think there are some unethical implications to that equation?

IN: No. If I were pushing you to stay, maybe.

CB: I can't quite figure you out, [redacted].

IN: You're no Monday crossword yourself, Casey.

CB: Touché.

IN: If you had to, what, or who, would you name for your nearly crippling fear of weight gain?

CB: Virginia Anne is the answer I think you are fishing for.

IN: Your mother. But you don't believe she has anything to do with this?

CB: If my commitment to keeping thin has something to do with seeing, then sure, you and I can spend some time trying to blame my mom.

IN: We aren't trying to blame anyone. We are trying to help everyone.

CB: Well, she has long since passed. There's not much we can do to help her.

IN: I'm sorry to hear that. Should we put our focus on someone or something else today?

CB: No. Let's press on. But ask it all. I can't say I'll be inclined to talk about her the next time you ask.

IN: Noted.

CB: Go on then.

IN: You don't believe your mother played some role in your preoccupation with weight, the way you look, or the regimen you have followed since the death of your father?

CB: I take full responsibility for who I am. That isn't to say that I don't recognize what she was. What she had. I have plenty of opinions about why she, like me, led a fairly successful life around body dysmorphia.

IN: I can't say that I believe there is such a thing as a successful life based on an eating disorder.

CB: I liked my life before I could see. You know, there is this whole, huge part of this country slothing around on weight totals that no respected scientist would ever quantify as healthy. What name do we have for them? Normal, average, just your everyday Joe and Jane Public.

IN: Aren't there extremes on both ends?

CB: I'm not talking about extremes. In the grand scheme of all things Anorexia Nervosa, I was far from the edge. Countless other humans sit on their imperfections, either hoping they will just magically go away, or pretending those flaws just don't matter. I suppose a few lucky ones are, in fact, completely unaware there is anything about themselves that needs addressing. Like me, my mother was quite cognizant of her own shortcomings. We worked to remedy them, those that we could.

IN: So, there were some similarities between you?

CB: What a dumb question. Of course, there were. I was born through her. She raised me before William's death, and well after his death too. But we are far from carbon copies.

IN: What specific differences would you point to?

CB: I work for my money. She did not. I readily admit that I am anorexic, she would never. And I am self-aware of my defects, but I don't go running around advertising them to the world. My mom had a nervous habit she couldn't help, something akin to a tic. Most people do not want to hear about your dribble chin at every dinner, every party, or any other random run-in. Even the people in your inner-circle.

IN: Dribble chin?

CB: Dribble chin. Turkey gullet. Frog's bubble. Chin Music. If you want the full Virginia Anne-effect, it is best to say any of the slang in a thicker, more effeminate Texas accent than my own. Dreee-ble cheeen. Turrrr-keee gull-it. Frawwwwwg's bubble. Cheeen mew-zik. Anyway, it's the fat skin pouch under a chin.

IN: I gathered.

CB: One can never be too sure.

IN: You have no accent.

CB: With the right motivation, no one has to.

IN: Sorry, please continue.

CB: I'm a grown man, operating independently of whatever disease my mother had or didn't have. I'm not running from my sickness, I'm running with it.

IN: To be clear, you don't believe your mother's possible anorexia has anything to do with your own?

CB: Who I am is a decision that I have made. If you want to blame someone, blame me.

IN: Some might suggest your view is a bit myopic.

CB: [redacted], you're in great shape. Some would say too skinny, I'm sure of that. While genetics is partly responsible for how well your body presents, your musculature suggests to me there is also an intentional effort. Is that the product of your mother's love? Your father's?

IN: Did your mother love you?

CB: With everything she had.

IN: Did you love your mother? Do you now?

CB: I would not be here without her. I know it's a lazily constructed sentiment. But I mean it.

IN: How so?

CB: She didn't just *have* me, she literally schemed me into the world.

IN: She planned to have you. How is that different from other women who think about starting a family?

CB: I was her idea of relationship glue. Not an accident, as she had my father believe, but part of a ploy to keep their union churning. She felt William was drifting away.

IN: Did she have good reason to believe that?

CB: My father was friendly to a fault. It'd be easy to misconstrue his pleasantries and affections for people, including women, as flirting. His peers were all having affairs, many quite openly. If he wasn't, he would have been the exception to the rich man's rule.

IN: Many couples mistakenly believe children will solve their interpersonal issues.

CB: Look, if I was just her idea of a Band-Aid, it took guts. I love her for that decision. I am aware she practiced cruel attention to the physical details of herself, her son, my father, and everyone else on this planet. She didn't have a filter for those opinions. She said what others think all the time, the criticisms most people are conditioned to keep to themselves. All this anonymous stuff on the internet? She'd have been livid. Not for what's being said, but because the people saying it don't have the stones to own it.

IN: Do you think your father only stayed with your mother because of you?

CB: He was very open about me being an addition to his life that he hadn't planned on... but he also assured me he was glad he hadn't insisted Virginia Anne get an abortion.

IN: How old were you when he told you that?

CB: I doubt there's an answer that'll ease your mind.

IN: (inaudible)

CB: Anyway, I wasn't aware of my mother's deception until after the accident.

IN: After you shot your dad?

CB: Yes.

IN: Do you believe your father was faithful to your mother?

CB: Until recently, I believed he had been.

IN: What changed your mind?

CB: I'd rather not say.

IN: But now you believe that he *had* been unfaithful?

CB: Yes… at least once.

IN: How did your mother handle William's death?

CB: She might have increased her reliance on alcohol and prescription medications, but there has always been a difference between the addict who can afford to be an addict and the addict who has to work for the money to stay an addict.

IN: And your relationship with your mother, did that change?

CB: Not into something else. But it did intensify. If that makes sense.

IN: When one parent dies unexpectedly, the bond between the remaining parent and children can intensify or it can weaken.

CB: Come 'ere, Hansum.

IN: This is you doing your mother, I take it?

CB: Come 'ere, Hansum. I need ta tell ya sumthin'. My mother committed fast and hard to the notion that with William gone, I was the other adult in the household. I was ten, but she had a whole lot of sumthins I guess she felt the new adult-me needed to know.

IN: Like what?

CB: She wasn't an angry woman, but she was a naturally unabashed blurter of uncomfortable truths. Some people confuse that kind of straightforwardness for being mean-spirited. Cruelty was not her motivation. If it had been, her tactless observations would still have been pardoned by most.

IN: Because of her money?

CB: My father's money, but no. My mom's classic veneer would have made her famous in the nineteen-twenties. Blunt criticism always lands softer when it's delivered by a natural beauty, even one who believed her neck should go under the knife. Good God, her knack for eloquently delivering damning realities to unsuspecting party guests was legendary. They loved her for it as much as they hated her for it.

IN: What types of things did she feel you should know?

CB: Some stuff you take to the grave, [redacted].

IN: If you don't feel like sharing, I'm not going to press.

CB: It's all tied up in some way or another, isn't it?

IN: What's that?

CB: Seeing.

IN: Perhaps.

CB: Next session you could tell me you think Lylian is the reason I can read the future. That reading the future has nothing to do with eating, calories, disorders or fuck-all else.

IN: Do you think Lylian is the reason you can see?

CB: No.

IN: It's your suggestion, I'm just—

CB: Love. I mean doesn't love move mountains?

IN: I'm not sure what this has to do with your mother?

CB: Don't fall in luv, Hansum. Marry for anythin' but. There's simply no logic to that per-tic-ler equation.

IN: Are you in love with Lylian?

CB: Isn't it obvious?

IN: I'd prefer to get it on record.

CB: I sparred for Cupid's cause, believe me.

IN: What do you mean?

CB: All of my mother's life-lessons had a way of meandering towards a general condemnation of coupling legally. When I got older, armed with only the experiences of boyhood crushes, I argued in favor of love as a reason for marriage. In fact, I went quite a bit further. I insisted that love was the only reason for living at all. In high school, I excelled at debate. I applied those skills to the arguments at home. I defended the absurd notions held by delusional romantics from across epochs. Something as seemingly trivial as a casual critique on that day's iced tea could end with us going blow to blow over the possibilities of love, soulmates, monogamy.

IN: Do you think Lylian loves you?

CB: Does it matter?

IN: You are scheduled to read tomorrow, do you still want to?

CB: Are you suggesting that I shouldn't?

IN: You've had some time away from it. You may not claim to feel better for it, but your energy level is proof enough. Maybe it's time to call it quits. Leave. With Lylian, of course.

CB: I want to read tomorrow.

IN: Can you read for us and refrain from evacuation after?

CB: Why?

IN: For your health. For your sanity. For Lylian, and, to be frank, for the research.

CB: I get the sense that there is something you are not telling me.

IN: The reading you did for us before the break—

CB: Your very, very long break.

IN: Yes, that one. Your last reading, before my break, it didn't come to pass. And, I think you already know that.

6

He is free to move, but not free to go.

Casey sits in a heavy slump at the end of another shabby motel bed under a popcorn ceiling. Twenty-four-seven news broadcasts from the television bolted to the dresser. The talking heads have opinions and those opinions have been diligently recycling at the top and bottom of each hour, at a volume just a few clicks above mute.

Lylian sits with her back to the swollen headboard. The distance between her and Casey is exaggerated by the faded pattern of blue lines on the frayed comforter. Their separation feels intentional and neither can hold eye contact with the other for more than a second or two. She casually nibbles fries from a styrofoam container. Each tiny bite is made with the earned calm of a woman who has lunched around a lifetime of horrible realities.

Casey's to-go box remains fastened beside him. The sloppy blue marker-made identification actually reads, "Cassidy." His meal is the only unopened delivery. The fragrance of fried everything radiates from the other six containers. Lunch for breakfast is over, and the stink of ketchup is tyrannical.

Thick curtains over the window have been pushed to one side. Beyond the aging pane, Cooper sits by the pool. He is stuffed into a teal plastic deckchair and holding court. His team now numbers four. Inside the room, his authority is an unsettling murmur. Jim, Daryl, and two new colleagues, a man and a woman, are huddled around him. Each agent is squeezed into a different chair, they look like circus bears playing tea-party, dressed in half-military fatigues and half-polo tops in a variety of absurd colors. Their camouflaged pants are belted by contraptions that suggest special ops and have to be a blind man's attempt at raising no eyebrows. Then again, it's Texas, they might just fit in. They could be gathered for an ex-forces' reunion, doing team-building vet exercises. They laugh heartily in between small bouts of listening to Cooper's directives, it sells that illusion well.

Inside, Casey breaks his silence.

"How long have you known, Lylian?"

"Only as long as you."

"I don't believe you," he quickly dismisses.

"Hey, I've been iffy on Cooper from day one. I'm not at all surprised that Hector hired him to execute a hit on David."

A playful jingle, promising happiness through the crunch of a new potato chip, sings out from the television. It's catchy and fun. Casey struggles to continue the conversation. Silent because he is confused, silent because he is displeased.

Lylian puts the few fries she has left to one side.

"In my experience, there are plenty of amenable agents working for the United States government," she says. "Don't be fooled by the mystique. These are blue collar guys collecting blue collar wages, and the cartels have always paid better."

"So, Diego's uncle, Hector, is basically what? Another David?"

"Basically. No one guy, no matter how clever they think they are, ever corners any black-market entirely. Is Hector also trafficking guns? Moving drugs? Guns and drugs? Who can say?"

"And Diego?" Casey cautiously asks.

"When Diego offered to help me, to look out for me and Ruby, and get us away from David, I took that chance. I trusted him—"

"He assaulted your daughter," Casey interrupts.

"—I trusted him, but that had nothing to do with his being a part of Hector's family. He was nice, until he wasn't."

Regret grabs Casey by the face. He carefully works his body closer to Lylian, stops an arm's length away, then leans toward her.

"I don't think you've quite grasped the seriousness of our situation. Hector has clearly been led to believe that David killed Diego. Or that David had him killed."

"So it would seem," Lylian says.

"Once David tells Cooper it was actually you who killed Diego, you don't think that'll be a problem?" he asks in a whisper. "What if Cooper shares that detail with Hector? Or at some point, David decides it's in his best interest to tell Hector you bashed his nephew's fucking brains out."

"Don't worry, David won't," she asserts, and in full volume.

"Why wouldn't he?"

"At this point, you'd be better off just letting things play out," she says with an edge. "Just because you lived in the shit with us for a few months, doesn't mean David's world is one you understand or will ever understand."

"Enlighten me, then."

Lylian looks out the window at Cooper. His gestures suggest the meeting is far from winding down. Another big laugh from the team rises outside, penetrates the thin walls. Lylian smiles, there is menace in its tilt.

"David is going to be absolutely thrilled when he finds out Hector thinks he was responsible for Diego's death."

"Why?"

"These fantasmas have their own rules. On the one hand, they operate as if they're just friendly competitors, hawking goods from cattycorner bodegas. And on the other, they look for any justifiable reason to fuck each other. Any little mistake to permit them to wipe that competition off the face of the earth."

"Are you saying that David has wanted Hector to think he offed Diego all along?"

"I can't say for sure. Was that the only reason he helped me take care of Diego's body? Maybe. He was excited, eager..." She seems to swallow a thought before continuing. "At the time, I thought it was because the favor put me under his thumb again. It doesn't matter. If Hector wants to start a beef, David will be happy to go to war."

"Or maybe he was excited because of me?" Casey blurts. "Surely offering to introduce him to a genuine prophet must have played a part in his cooperating."

Lylian looks away from Casey and struggles to come back to him. Her face has gone limp.

"Lyl?"

"Maybe."

"Now that I've said it aloud, even I don't believe meeting me had fuck-all to do with David helping you."

Lylian stays quiet.

"Is there something you aren't telling me, Lyl?"

"You said something, at the last hotel while you were eating. I'd never heard you say it before."

"It is time? I was just riffing psychic babble—"

"Not that bullshit, before that. You were mumbling, How will the world know you."

"Did I?"

"You did."

"Hmm, okay. I'll have to take your word for it."

"It's an unusual thing to say."

"It's something my father used to ask me. I don't vocalize it often, but it lives in my head rent free. Why?"

"Is it a quote from someone famous?"

"I don't think so."

"You aren't the first person I've heard ask it."

The door swings wide open. The West Texas heat is immediate. Cooper and his team rumble into the room, the smell of skin baked by sun enters too. This space wasn't designed for a crowd. The door shuts and the room instantly feels six times smaller.

"Please tell me you aren't trying to concoct some ass-backwards attempt to escape," Cooper says with a hard stare.

"Wouldn't dream of it," Lylian says. "I'm all in. Would it be alright if I used the bathroom though?"

She stands, trying to grab Casey's hand while heading there, but Cooper moves quick. He stops just shy of striking distance and his new proximity is enough to pause her momentum.

"In a minute," he says. "Plenty of time to take a leak before we head out."

Behind him, the team unpacks black bags. They grab pieces of weapons to assemble and jockey for the room's only chair. The woman wins. Daryl and Jim drop themselves to the floor, but the new guy isn't shy, and his magnitude comes down on the bed with a thump. The force of his ass hitting the mattress sends Casey's uneaten lunch to the floor. The food lies piled upon itself next to its open container. The last thing the room needed was the smell of a Monte Cristo sandwich.

"Five second rule still applies," Cooper says.

Casey ignores the ridicule. He hops from the bed and puts himself between Cooper and Lylian, puffy chest and all.

"Goddammit, Cooper. Honor our bet. Let me read!"

The ask is convincingly threatening. The squad looks up

from their task, each putting eyes on Casey without pausing from the assembly of their weapons.

"No time, Casey."

The team obediently goes back to readying their tools.

Lylian steps within reach of Casey, puts her hands on his shoulders and grips him tight.

"I agree. Fuck the future," she says. "I'm no longer interested. All that matters is what we do right now."

Cooper reaches into his rear pocket and pulls out a tiny black-flip phone. He dangles it in front of Lylian as he steps closer.

"Here's your phone," he says. "Make the call."

"I already made the only phone call that matters, Cooper."

"No, you haven't," he says. "It's time to quit fucking around."

The television pronounces the broadcast has reached the top of yet another hour.

Lylian's fingers dig deep into Casey.

A single bullet shatters glass. It tears through the fabric of fire-retardant curtains and buries itself deep into the drywall. A warning shot that has disappeared into the history of the motel's skeleton.

With a last-laugh glint in her eyes, Lylian practically sings, "You're right, Cooper, enough fucking around. I didn't make a call... it was actually a text."

Everyone else is still processing the single shot. Lylian's perfect moment is brief. Its tranquility is interrupted by the repetitive pops of more gunfire from outside. Each new bullet races into the room with a whistle.

Lylian rips Casey backward, forcing his body to the floor as she falls on top of him. Behind the bed's commercial box frame, they cling to the carpet beneath their hands. She pushes every bit of her weight into him.

Cooper drops Lylian's phone and launches himself to the ground. The others aren't so quick.

The bullets attack like hornets, find their way immediately into the necks, heads, and abdomens of Cooper's team, save Jim. The three giants fall fast. Quick casualties, their bodies hit the floor with thunder. Crumpled, they look small and weak. Their last contribution to the world? More stains.

"You bitch!" Cooper shouts.

Lylian grins, then she rolls herself off of Casey. She positions her body to his right. His eyes look for answers. She mouths, *Are you okay?* He nods as best as he can with his head glued to the carpet.

"We're going to be fine," she says over the noise, and it sounds believable.

She points in the direction of the bathroom. Though Casey tries to protest any additional advance, she pushes at his legs, encouraging him to move.

He army crawls toward the corner of the bed's frame. The sound of glass crashing on cheap tile rings from the bathroom. Casey freezes. He holds his position, then makes an earnest attempt to peer around the footboard. From there, he tries to assess who is left.

"Fuck it," Cooper says. He rolls into a crouch behind the dresser. "Jim! Shoot the traffic passing the motel! Shoot at anything that moves!"

Behind a table turned on its top's edge, Jim responds to the command with a steely wink.

The sound of Jim and Cooper's guns pervade the room as Lylian continues to push at Casey's feet. He worms his way forward, curling around the wall's end, then shuffling over the bathroom door's threshold. The attack from outside seemingly doubles. Shards of mirror and broken porcelain litter the tile between Casey and the protection of a cast iron tub. He holds one arm out in front of himself, batting the debris back and forth across the floor like a fleshy broom. He rakes at the sharp pieces, taking on more of them than he pushes away. As he shuffles toward the tub, the remaining jagged fragments drag along for the ride. The assault over his head is relentless, but he stops just long enough to check if Lylian is behind. She taps at the bottom of his legs, slapping at his calves, points fiercely at the tub. With a blood-strewn limb, he reaches blindly for the basin's edge. He pulls himself up and balances on the rim, flops himself into the bottom, then swings an arm outside of the tub to locate Lylian. Her tiny hand grabs his first.

Outside of the bathroom, there is a distinct boom. It bears no resemblance to any of the percussion that had proceeded it. The blast shakes the wall's fixtures loose and separates the plumbing from its aging seals. Water spits and hisses in fits from slivers in the exposed pipe couplings underneath the sink.

Lylian pops from the floor, drops herself into the tub and on top of Casey. Their bodies work to stay well within the protective space. She makes eye contact with him. She doesn't cry, she doesn't scream. If anything, she carries the certainty of someone who placed a big bet on an event they had personally seen to fixing.

The steady zip of endless slugs ends. Aside from the wheeze of water spilling to the floor, the room has gone silent. Even the television's voices have been put to bed. The sour mix of take-out, sex, bleach, and human sweat has been evicted. The metallic stench of blood and gunpowder reign supreme.

"Stay put," Cooper shouts from somewhere on the other side of the bathroom wall. The command feels weak, as if he were drunk.

There is another thwack, then the hard roll of a sheet steel cylinder tumbling off of the dresser. The canister falls to the floor, making an unimpressive clunk as it meets the carpet. Lylian pushes her body deep into Casey's.

There is a click.

There is a fizz.

Cooper cries out, "Casey, cover your—"

His warning is interrupted by the sick sound of a hard boot slammed into his face.

A chemical haze billows through the bathroom door. The smoke thins and thickens as it dances with the suction of the exhaust fan above it. Through the milky vapor, a shape donning head-to-toe black appears.

David winks at Casey from behind the protection of his service-issue gas mask.

Casey tries to get up, but the incapacitating agent has taken hold. Lylian weakly presses him into the tub. Before they are both out, she puts the heat of her mouth to his ear.

"Don't worry. He won't kill us. I think you might be family."

Subject: CASEY BANKS
Interviewer: [redacted]
Date of Interview: 12/13/2015
CB=Casey Banks, IN=Interviewer

IN: This interview is being recorded. The time is 10:15AM. How are you feeling this morning, Casey?

CB: Optimistic.

IN: Really?

CB: Should I change my answer?

IN: No. Not if optimistic was the truth.

CB: It's true enough.

IN: Is there anything in particular that has you feeling hopeful?

CB: Well, I didn't say hopeful.

IN: Is there a difference?

CB: In my opinion, yes. Though it is probably very slim.

IN: So today we are playing word games.

CB: All business, then. Okay.

IN: Is there something specific that has you feeling optimistic?

CB: That feeling has passed.

IN: Fine. I'll move on.

CB: Chicken.

IN: Your sense of humor has returned. I suppose I *should* be happy about that.

CB: You aren't?

IN: Aren't what?

CB: You aren't happy that my sense of humor has returned? You said that you *should* be.

IN: Gotcha. Of course, I'm happy about it. It's very promising.

CB: (laughter)

IN: It's good to hear you laugh, Casey. Truly.

CB: I am thrilled you approve.

IN: You read yesterday. I'm told you did not self-induce vomiting directly after reporting your vision.

CB: I am a man of my word.

IN: And I believe that. Still, I have to ask, did you vomit or try to vomit when you returned to your room?

CB: I think you would know.

IN: And why is that?

CB: Cameras.

IN: There are no hidden cameras in your room, nor Lylian's—

CB: I'm kidding. I know there are no cameras. Trust me, we looked. I thought maybe the smell, or lack thereof, might be all the evidence you needed.

IN: I doubt the smells from the exited meal would linger in this room long enough for my nose to take note.

CB: Lucky you. It's been weeks since I've hurled, but I can conjure the scents on demand.

IN: For the record though, you didn't throw up after yesterday's reading, correct?

CB: I did not.

IN: I'm glad—

CB: To what end though?

IN: There are several positive outcomes, I'm sure.

CB: Fine, name just one of them.

IN: I can't speak for the hopes of the entire team—

CB: Jesus, [redacted].

IN: Speaking only for myself, I want a conclusion here that sees you better prepared to handle life outside of here. Is that a sufficiently worthy end? I'm guessing you'll say no.

CB: I can work with that.

IN: (inaudible)

CB: What's that sound for?

IN: You can be extremely frustrating. That's unprofessional of me to say, but, well, I've said it, haven't I?

CB: I'm not offended.

IN: I can't imagine there is much left that would offend you.

CB: I certainly hope that is not true.

IN: Shall we move on?

CB: Yes.

IN: You didn't throw up after the reading yesterday. That's progress. How far into the subject's future had you been asked to travel?

CB: A week.

IN: Great. I suppose we will know what effect, if any, not purging had on yesterday's reading roughly a week from now.

CB: And then what?

IN: I'm not sure what it is you want to hear.

CB: When I came here, I wanted answers. Unless I am mistaken, you and the team have none.

IN: It's not an exact science.

CB: It hardly feels like science at all.

IN: There are answers. There are always answers, sometimes it can just take a while to find them.

CB: Unless this program starts to pay, in cash, I think it might be time to call it quits. I don't mean to be rude. I realize you aren't in charge here.

IN: You are anxious to get back out there so that you can start making money again?

CB: Money is not a forever solution, but in the near term, I think more of it could be helpful to us.

IN: It's almost as if you believe more money is the key to changing your future. And altering your future is something I'm not certain you believe is even possible.

CB: Fair enough.

IN: You have money. Some might say a lot of money.

CB: That's my father's money.

IN: The funds I'm referencing are in bank accounts in your name. Six figure sums across a variety of financial institutions.

CB: Family money—

IN: Your family is dead. You have no living relatives that I'm aware of. I understand that your fortune is predominately made up of an inheritance that was left to you when your mother passed, but the entirety of that legacy now belongs solely to you. It just—

CB: I don't expect you to understand.

IN: What does money *you earn* guarantee you in the near term?

CB: A more normal life.

IN: A more normal life is what you want?

CB: Yes.

IN: Your life has been anything but normal, wouldn't you agree?

CB: Sure.

IN: If normal exists, what makes you think you are ready for that kind of benign existence?

CB: I am tired. At a certain point, isn't normal what everyone surrenders to?

IN: I don't want to make assumptions here. Your projection of normal living, does that include recovery from the eating disorders you have, old and new?

CB: I think there are healthier ways for me to maintain the physical appearance I desire.

IN: Lylian is very thin.

CB: Yes, she is.

IN: Would it bother you if, over time, she became heavier?

CB: She wouldn't.

IN: Don't the people who choose a normal lifestyle tend to drift further and further away from the type of appearance that you are fond of?

CB: She won't.

IN: There's a better than forty-percent chance that she will.

CB: If I believed she was going to be in my life a long time— long enough for me to see her decide to succumb to the pull of this world's literally growing zeitgeist—I guess it would be of some concern.

IN: You think Lylian is going to leave you?

CB: Who can say?

IN: Well, you can say. Maybe you've already seen that she's going to leave you. Have you?

CB: It is just as likely that I too am using established data and odds to speculate about the length of our relationship.

IN: Ever the actuary.

CB: Do you know how long the average romantic relationship lasts in this country?

IN: A little under three years.

CB: Lylian leaving me doesn't require psychic powers. The chances of her ending our relationship are better than the odds you just tossed at me regarding obesity.

IN: You are dodging the question. Have you foreseen Lylian deciding to end things with you?

CB: No.

IN: If that's true, do you recognize how unhealthy it is to exist in a relationship that you've already decided isn't going to last?

CB: I hardly think that's what I am doing.

IN: Your own feelings for Lylian might fade too. In this normal life you are pining for, isn't it equally likely that, at some point, the way you feel about her will end and you will leave her?

CB: Not because she got fat.

IN: Have you foreseen yourself deciding to end things with Lylian?

CB: No.

IN: You don't sound so sure.

CB: (inaudible)

IN: Fine. You've admitted to traveling to parts of her timeline. Did any of those visions reveal that your relationship with Lylian had ended?

CB: Not exactly.

IN: I feel sorry for you, Casey.

CB: Don't.

IN: I can't help it, I do.

CB: Then help me, [redacted]. Tell me what you know.

IN: Sharing anything the team might have learned from our interviews or the readings' observations is considered risky.

CB: How?

IN: To put it simply: we don't want you thinking about why you can read, we just want you to keep reading.

CB: And if I refuse to perform any more visions?

IN: We control what we can control. You are always free to leave. I feel like a broken record on that part.

CB: At some point, though, you will share that information?

IN: Learning why you can do what you do... is that the real reason for your continued cooperation?

CB: One of the reasons.

IN: Lylian's safety, Ruby's wellbeing, these are others?

CB: (inaudible)

IN: Quite the contrary, I think it's admirable. I truly do.

7

He is one of six and on the move.

Half the cabal in the bed of the box truck are captors. The other half are captives. The bodies of Jim, Daryl, and Cooper's other two collaborators were collected and thrown into another truck. That vehicle went its own direction minutes into the ride.

The skin on either side of Casey's nose is raw, a dark purplish pink from the exposure to the chemical assault an hour ago. His tawny eyelids struggle to rise past half-mast, and his deep breaths have an almost mechanical grind to them.

The wheezes Lylian makes with every third inhale offer a disturbing harmony. She sits gracelessly beside him. Both are doing what little they can to stay upright upon an unforgiving wood bench.

David is handling the fickleness of the motion more expertly than the rest, but only Cooper is stock-still. No longer a mammoth force, his body is stuffed awkwardly between the pews, hands bound. His once unflappable will is shallowly buried into the pebble-pocked surface of the truck's bed, a big-game trophy, pinned under the heavy combat boot on David's left foot.

"Can I be honest with you both?" David asks.

Lylian's face reboots. She heard his question, her eyes answer, *fuck off.*

"When I *let* you two run, let being the key word here," he says, "I truly believed our next get-together would be consensual. Perhaps foolishly, I was banking on it."

The confession lingers. For a moment, he turns his attention to the inhospitable details of the dusty hold hosting their reunion. He sighs emphatically, seems genuinely disappointed in the location.

"This isn't at all what I had in mind," he says. His sadness slides into a crooked grin. "But it's the company that counts, right?"

"Bullshit," Lylian manages in between rasps that have no tempo. "Utter bullshit, and you know it."

"No, no, it's true. Don't get me wrong. Your decision to leave the ranch stung. It hurt me very deeply," David insists. "But, as one does, I put myself in your shoes—his, and yours—and I think I understand your reasons for fleeing."

Lylian inflates her posture, but the ruggedness of the ride makes it difficult to hold a threatening stance while seated. She leans forward, puts her face as close to David as she can without toppling, and keeps the position just long enough to spit on him.

"You wouldn't let us go. Not on purpose."

David stifles a laugh and wipes away her saliva from his cheek.

"What, then? We are to believe that you, on a bike, and Casey, on foot, covered miles of remote desert—desert patrolled by my drones I might add—and somehow skillfully evaded my men as they searched for you, night and day?"

"We had help," Casey offers as he sheepishly nods at Cooper's body.

David's eyes are no longer puckish. They are ice blue fire.

"Who? Him?" He raises the potential force of his boot over Cooper. He strikes down bluntly into his thoracic vertebrae, just below his neck. The punctuation lands with a horrendous thud. "Please... you can't honestly believe that."

Other than an involuntary gasp, Cooper remains out cold.

Casey looks away as Lylian shakes her head in disgust. David throws himself over the aisle and clasps his hands behind Casey's neck. His head goes down hard as David drags it toward the floor, demanding a more personal observation of Cooper.

"Is this your hero?" he asks, then shoves Casey back into his seat. "You did have help, that much is true. Me. *I* was your help."

His laughter is ugly and uncomfortably long.

Lylian springs from the bench, but her swings fall short. In her condition, it is hard to dominate David's moment. She fights for a footing that leaves her standing long enough to land one clumsy punch.

"Where's Ruby?" she shouts as she finds her balance. "What have you done with her?"

The two soldiers at David's left grin eagerly, begging for permission to jump Lylian. He waves the men off as he pushes his chest into the fat of her palms, absorbing her blows. She loses steam, and he captures her wrists in his hand. From that iron grip, he throws Lylian's full weight into the crease where wooden bench meets metal frame. The crown of her head bounces off the box truck's wall.

David makes a point of dusting himself off.

"What the fuck, Lylian?" he says. He pulls a nylon zip tie from out of a backpack on the floor and waves it in front of her. "We don't need these, do we?"

Though she finds some semblance of an equilibrium, she doesn't answer and her eyes are shut tight.

"I didn't think so," David says. He returns the restraints gently into his bag. "Ruby is fine, of course. Better than fine.

Much safer with me than she'd be under the protection of either of you."

The snarl of three additional trucks joins the rumble. Casey's eyes awaken, but the momentum of the ride slows and his hope goes dark.

"Oh no," David says, altering his voice to sound like a child. "Did you think it was the good guys come to save you from da big bad wolf?"

He smirks, but it doesn't take. His prior euphoria seems dented by the intrusion.

In the near distance, dogs bark effusively. It's the kind of Pavlovian hullabaloo one associates with a kennel's pack realizing the hand that feeds is oh-so-close to home.

"Where's Marion, then?" Lylian asks in a broken voice. She can barely keep her eyes open, but lands what stare she can on David. "Did you kill her?"

Their stand-off isn't long. He winks at her, big, then turns to Casey.

"How will the world know me?" he asks.

Casey's expression glitches, his brain threatening to crash.

"Come on, Casey," David says. "Help me out. How will the world know me? Especially when my only biographer over here is so clearly biased."

David seems tickled to wait on a response.

"How will the world know you?" Casey meekly repeats.

"I think he's catching on, Lylian. Even if you never did."

Lylian studies Casey's face before turning back to David who is pointing to his own features, hands held exaggeratedly high, frozen in pose as if someone's about to snap a Polaroid.

"Cut the crap, David," she says, but it's obvious his and Casey's physical similarities have cemented.

After all, a nose is a nose, even if it lives a fat life or thin.

"Only you could ruin this moment," David says as he brings

his hands to his lap. "She's not great with surprises, Casey. It can be... very aggravating, to put it lightly."

Casey is steadfast in his own silent disbelief.

"If you have any feelings left for me, you'll let us—"

"Let you what, Lylian? Go?" David asks. "Why would I do that again?"

"Because—"

"Lylian, let me speak please. When you decided to run with Diego—to trust Diego over me—I should've had someone keep an eye on you. I knew that. It was in my gut. I didn't need that fucker to hurt Ruby to know that. And I'll regret having let you momentarily take charge of her welfare for the rest of my life."

His voice is no longer playful.

"At this point, I think it's pretty obvious who the better parent is."

"Did you kill my mom, David?"

"Unlike someone in here, I don't execute family."

"Did you?" she repeats.

"Have *you* ever seen me kill anyone?" he asks Casey.

Before Casey can answer, Cooper rotates onto his side. Half his face becomes visible. From behind the bubbles of saliva percolating around his lips, nonsensical words try in earnest to escape. David puts a quick end to the jumble's formation with another violent thrust of a hard rubber sole into the man's jaw.

"I'm sorry. The question was for you specifically, Casey. Have you ever actually seen *me* kill anyone? Personally?"

Casey doesn't take any time to think, he just answers.

"No."

"But you, Casey," he continues, "You have killed before? Slayed a man by your own hand."

The truck brakes. Everyone grabs for something to hold as the last sharp turn does a number on their poise.

"No, not on purpose."

"No, of course not," David says as he leans closer to Casey. "I was only nine years old at the time, but I read the headlines. Tragic hunting accident leaves beloved Texas icon dead, survived by his wife and *only* son... or so the details claimed."

The sound of the other vehicles fades. The dogs' excitement is closer.

"I've always wondered though, was it really an accident?" David asks. The truck comes to a complete stop. "Or maybe you had a good reason... maybe I was the reason you killed William that day."

David doesn't allow for anything more. He stands and swings the rear doors open before anyone else can speak.

"Home sweet home," he offers. "Mother and daughter reunited at last. What a joyous occasion, am I right?"

David's soldiers waste no time picking up Cooper's body. They heave his bulk down to two other men, each has a rifle hanging from one shoulder. As they haul Cooper away, David hops out, then turns to hold a hand up to help Lylian step down from the rig. She takes it willingly and jumps to the ground.

From behind the shorter of two chain-link perimeter fences that surround the estate, Ruby delivers all the punch Lylian needs to break the spell of her lingering muddle.

"Mommy! Mommy! Estás aquí! Estás aquí!"

David holds Lylian's hand tight, refusing to release her. He alone controls access to the tiny blur bouncing about the penned yard a stone's throw away. He squeezes her fingers, increases the compression, but Lylian refuses to show him the gratitude his leash on her is meant to produce. Her tenacity is on full display. Without a single word, she's begging him to break the bones in her fingers.

"For fuck's sake, just let her go." Casey says.

David's clutch reluctantly opens and Lylian doesn't waste a second. She dashes up the hill toward her daughter.

"Mi muñequita, mi muñequita! Mommy's home!"

David sighs hard, then turns to Casey who stands at the

hold's interior edge. Casey watches wistfully as Lylian and Ruby nearly fall to the ground from the impact of their reunion.

"I missed you, Casey," David interrupts, breaking the moment.

"You missed what I can do for you."

"In time, I think you'll come to realize I value family. I mean that sincerely." He puts his hand into the air to help Casey down. "Even if that family once took the only thing that mattered to me away from me... for good."

"It was an accident—"

"Plenty of time to tell me your story later, Big Brother."

Subject: CASEY BANKS
Interviewer: [redacted]
Date of Interview: 12/21/2015
CB=Casey Banks, IN=Interviewer

IN: This interview is being recorded. The time is 9:35AM. Good morning, Casey.

CB: Hello, [redacted].

IN: You are looking well today.

CB: Thanks.

IN: I don't want to get this session off on the wrong foot, but how are you doing—

CB: —with not vomiting?

IN: Yes.

CB: Fine.

IN: Is everything alright? You seem terse.

CB: I'm having a "why me" day.

IN: Well, I can assure you, you aren't alone in this.

CB: I beg to differ.

IN: I'm here.

CB: You are paid to be here. And only twice a week I might add.

IN: Would you like to increase the number of visits we have in a week? I am open to the idea.

CB: You are the only reason I am still here.

IN: What about Lylian?

CB: I misspoke. You are the only reason *we* are still here.

IN: Clearly that's not what I meant.

CB: Mm-hmm.

IN: In one of our prior conversations, I got the distinct impression that you were putting yourself through all of this to keep Lylian safe, to keep Ruby safe.

CB: That remains true.

IN: Has something changed?

CB: I think I have always known they would both be better off without my help. And without me.

IN: I wouldn't be so blunt with just any patient, but you are more self-aware than most. May I?

CB: Shoot.

IN: You know as well as I do that whatever feelings of inadequacy you are having are just that, feelings. I doubt Lylian would still be here if she didn't want to be with you.

CB: I already said I was having a "why me" day. It would be nice to be given the space to run with that feeling for a bit.

IN: Fair enough.

CB: So, why me?

IN: There are others like you. Many, in fact.

CB: I take it you mean others with eating disorders.

IN: Exactly. I've wanted to ask you for some time, would you be willing to do group therapy when you leave here? There are men's only groups I could put you in touch with.

CB: You really don't care that I can see, do you?

IN: I might have. But, now? I can't say that I do.

CB: I doubt that news is going to sit well with "the team."

IN: It may not.

CB: I admire that you don't seem to care.

IN: About your ability to see?

CB: No. About them. About what the team wants from me or what they may eventually ask of you.

IN: You believe they have sinister motivations?

CB: [redacted], do you have an idea why you are here?

IN: You're upset because last time, I told you they were paying me quite a bit to be here.

CB: No, I mean, do you know *what* you are doing here?

IN: Do you, Casey? Do you know what *you* are doing here?

CB: Fine, I'll answer first: Yes, absolutely.

IN: Okay, then. What is it that you are doing here?

CB: Killing time until the inevitable.

IN: Don't play coy, answer the question.

CB: I came to see who it was that I'd be saving.

IN: Oh, I see.

CB: Don't take this the wrong way, but, no, you don't.

IN: Whoever your true self is, Casey, I promise you, it's someone worth saving.

CB: I'm going to be fine. I'm not worried about me.

IN: I think that's clearly part of the—

CB: You said you are married, [redacted]?

IN: Did I?

CB: When you got back from Thanksgiving, yeah. Do you love your husband?

IN: I don't see how's that relevant, but, yes.

CB: You love him, or *loved* him and are just still with him?

IN: My relationship with my husband is in no way similar to how you define your parents' relationship.

CB: I don't doubt that. You told me that you had a child as well.

IN: Yes, *children* actually. Two. A boy and a girl.

CB: (inaudible)

IN: Are you alright?

CB: I'm fine. And I'm sorry. You've been very good to me, [redacted]. I think I'm just stir-crazy.

IN: That's understandable.

CB: Are there questions for me today? From the team?

IN: There are. But we can talk about anything you'd like.

CB: I want to go ahead and continue with whatever it is they have tasked you with.

IN: Even if the questions are about Lylian?

CB: Even then.

IN: When did you first ask Lylian out?

CB: I didn't.

IN: She asked you out, then?

CB: Shocking, I know.

IN: How so?

CB: Women don't ask this out.

IN: You're selling yourself short.

CB: I realize there are plenty of examples of men with ugly mugs riding atop of bean poles who have cover-girl girlfriends. Musicians, actors, Silicon Valley billionaires, it's not a short list. These men have money. These men have talent. Are these same men on any woman's radar without either of those carrots?

IN: Lylian saw something in you.

CB: Or Lylian saw *someone* in me.

IN: You reminded her of someone, you mean?

CB: Subconsciously, I think. Though it's kind of difficult to see anything past a real-world manifestation of a Tim Burton creation.

IN: You can be charming. That can do a lot of heavy lifting.

CB: Even if that were true, I'm not sure how much of my glowing personality would have been discernible for Lylian from my daily *thank you, this is perfect, I'll see you tomorrow.*

IN: You were kind.

CB: It is in short supply.

IN: You were attracted to her. She probably sensed that.

CB: Every Blitz Café regular was attracted to her, male or female, single or in a relationship. Some people seem unattainable, even if they are just slinging coffee for minimum wage. Trust me, there was nothing unique about my being attracted to Lyl. I used to sit in the shadows of the café, nursing a black iced coffee, just to watch suitor after suitor, the more forward-than-me variety, crash and burn spectacularly.

IN: Were you working up the courage to ask her out?

CB: Inaction was my plan.

IN: Stalking is hardly considered inaction.

CB: Well, I never followed her.

IN: By definition, I'm not sure you have to.

CB: Fair enough. I was stalking her then.

IN: And at some point, she asked you out?

CB: In me, I think she saw someone else.

IN: You seem to believe that. As if she's mentioned it specifically.

CB: A different version of someone she had already loved.

IN: Her father?

CB: She didn't know her father.

IN: Oh, no?

CB: He was deported when she was very young. They sent him back to Honduras, and he went missing shortly thereafter. My understanding is that most of her childhood was a long list of uncle-so-and-sos.

IN: Okay, then. Are we talking about David?

CB: You sound as though you'd be quick to dismiss it if I was.

IN: That's simply not true.

CB: Maybe I'm hoping you *will* be quick to tell me I'm being absurd.

IN: I'm happy to entertain the notion. What, if any, evidence do you have to support it?

CB: Nothing on paper. Nothing real. Not yet.

IN: Okay, give me something flimsy.

CB: One of the very first things Lylian said to me, about me, was, "You seem like the wouldn't harm a fly type. Or maybe the *couldn't* harm a fly type. There's a difference."

IN: That sounds like she was seeking someone who was the exact opposite of David.

CB: I can tell you that it didn't sound like a guy I wanted to be.

IN: That's an entirely different issue altogether.

CB: If you say so.

IN: Did you feel she was calling you weak?

CB: No. I think she meant it as a compliment.

IN: When she said that, was she aware you were anorexic?

CB: No. Keep in mind I wasn't this thin then. Thin, but not like this. She thought I was just very fit.

IN: She learned you were anorexic at some point though?

CB: Sure, but I didn't start the relationship with, "Hey, how's it going? Soooooo, I'm an anorexic."

IN: That's understandable. I assume she didn't immediately own up to being in hiding from her ex.

CB: Well, that assumption sucks.

IN: She did tell you.

CB: On our first date, before we'd even made it to the bar.

IN: Was that information unsettling?

CB: I think I found her honesty refreshing, though the subject matter was dark.

IN: Perhaps you were attracted to the potential dangers of a situation like hers.

CB: Or maybe I felt my own fucked-up life would pale in comparison when laid against the particulars of her own.

IN: A kind of misery loves company type of thing?

CB: It's a platitude for a good reason. I knew violence once. Lylian had known it often.

IN: Not a traditional bedrock of a solid relationship, but I think I understand. Had you dated much before Lylian?

CB: Here and there, but mostly no.

IN: Let's table the why behind Lylian's attraction to you for a moment. I'd like to better understand your attraction to her. Would that be alright?

CB: I'm not sure this will make sense, but I was instantly comfortable around her.

IN: Can you give me an example?

CB: Our first dinner together, I let myself eat. A lot.

IN: (inaudible)

CB: Why are you smiling?

IN: It's just nice to hear, Casey.

CB: It was nice. Don't get me wrong, physically, I was miserable. Truly stuffed.

IN: I can imagine.

CB: It's all so fucked though.

IN: How do you mean?

CB: Haven't we talked about this before?

IN: I'm not sure. What are you referring to when you say, it's all so fucked?

CB: Two weeks of dates, two weeks of that on-a-cloud feeling. Eating, running, eating, running, repeat, repeat, repeat.

IN: It was during that time that you had your first vision?

CB: Yes.

IN: Can you describe how that played out?

CB: I'll admit, I let myself go overboard that night. I was eating to make up for years.

IN: Totally understandable.

CB: We were both too drunk to drive, it was a long walk to my house, but I convinced Lyl it'd be good for our digestion.

IN: And you had that first vision while walking?

CB: Yes.

IN: How long had it been since you'd taken your last bite?

CB: Actually, we'd taken cake to go, so I was still eating.

IN: And?

CB: And nothing, and everything. It just came to me.

IN: I get that, but what was it like? What did that vision feel like?

CB: I lost all focus on what Lylian and I were talking about. I felt lightheaded and I thought it was the booze, maybe all the sugar. I tried to shake it off, but before I could find my way back into the conversation, I just... saw what I saw.

IN: When did you realize it was a legitimate peek into the future?

CB: When we watched it happen just down the street from me.

IN: Which was when?

CB: The very next day.

IN: What happened?

CB: The bus blew the red light, t-boned the car crossing the intersection. Demolished the hatchback on impact.

IN: Accidents happen all the time, what made you so sure it was the accident you'd seen the night before?

CB: In my vision, the driver's head had been severed clean off of her body, flown through the air, and landed at the furry feet of a Brussels Griffon out for a walk. In my vision, the only passenger in the car was a young boy not nearly old enough to be in the front seat of any car, let alone an airbag-less beater. Should I go on?

IN: No.

CB: What I had seen was now what I saw, follow?

IN: That's truly heartbreaking.

CB: And I spared you the more detailed horrors, [redacted].

IN: Lylian was with you?

CB: Yes. I was visibly shaken. She walked with me to my place, came up, and I told her immediately. I believe I had referred to it as a premonition.

CB: And she believed you?

IN: No. Of course, not.

CB: How did you convince her?

IN: It wasn't pretty.

8

He is well-dressed, but beaten.

Casey stands in the compound's rear courtyard, not far from the oversized teak table made ready for a group dinner. The table can easily seat ten, but there are only chairs enough for six. Two on either long side and one at each shorter end. The blood-orange sun works its magic on the white linen and porcelain place settings. Without it, there wouldn't be a hint of color to the decor. Even the chairs are supremely pale. The design of it all suggest civility.

He is alone and unsteady, bathed and wearing fresh clothes. Loose, colorless, and without a pattern. Casey could stand in as a groomsman at some heroin-chic wedding and not a single guest would be the wiser. If he were a pound lighter, the swift West Texas breeze might whip him up and over the courtyard's stone walls.

He studies his reflection in the shallow pool of a fountain. The robust gurgle accents the gentle mutilation of his disfigurement. The lines that define the contours of his face don't look as sharp dancing upon the water's unsettled surface. He runs a single thin finger along his sinking flesh, traces the collapse under the bone running between an eye socket and his frown's corner. He leaves his protrusion there, pushing the digit deeper into one cheek, as if he were hoping to pop his whole head like a balloon.

Through an oversized arch at the farthest corner of the courtyard, Lylian appears. She is gorgeous and uncomfortable. It is doubtful the immodest red party dress she is pulling at was her selection. Without making a sound, the garb disturbs the fatigue of the desert around them.

She scans the interior perimeter, high and low, entering reluctantly. At the center of the garden, her pace is more resolute. Her grin grows gingerly as she nears Casey, but it's no less potent for having been born under duress. Her happiness to see him has no effect and her smile stalls. Its corners fall as she slowly exhales into a standstill.

Casey doesn't bother to lift his head. Atop the herringbone pattern of red brick, the two of them are on pause. She bites at her bottom lip as he continues his long look at her feet, bare as his own, but less skeletal.

"No shoes for you either?" he asks.

The quip lies somewhere between playful and ill-at-ease.

"Nope. And they took the ones I came in on too," Lylian says, trying to sound upbeat.

"Same."

Only the wind speaks for a while. Lylian waits on his expression, examines his face in silence. It's as if she needs an indication from him, any small physical hint of his wanting her to resume her approach. He offers none. He leaves the sweep of uncertainty between them.

Casey asks, "How's Ruby?" It sounds sincere.

"She's sleeping," Lylian answers. "My mother is here too. Both are fine, but both are understandably confused. Ruby more so than Marion."

The news brings the bend of joy to Casey's face, but it

quickly collapses. The inward loll of his ashen cheeks seems deeper and his blue eyes could pass for gray.

Lylian takes a small step toward Casey as he simultaneously reasserts their distance by walking his own small step backwards.

"How are you?" she asks, trying to hide a minor tremble in her voice. She doesn't sound afraid, she sounds concerned.

"I'm fine, Lylian," Casey says with weak anger. "Just fine."

The clang of kitchen help momentarily rises above the purl of the fountain. Though the commotion fades as quickly as it had interrupted, it's a good indication this private moment won't be a long one.

Lylian inches one foot in front of the other. Casey has no space left to retreat, the muscles of his calves dig into the fountain's border.

"Casey, if you've already seen where this is going, you need to tell me now."

"Where do you want it to go, Lylian?"

His question unnerves.

"What the fuck is that supposed to mean?"

Shoed steps in an adjacent corridor echo about the courtyard, prompting Casey to leave her question unanswered. Neither dares speak again until the sounds of the stroll are distant.

"What are you trying to say?" she asks, softer, with a feigned politeness.

Casey steps into her. Their bodies are no more than an inch apart. They are held together by the anticipation of his answer.

"*You* contacted David," he quietly reminds her. "At this point, we're only here again because of you. Our current predicament must be exactly what you wanted it to be."

Lylian pauses, fidgets through disappointment, then says, "Cooper would have fucked this up way worse." She is even-keeled. "At least now we have a chance at survival."

"Whose survival?"

"Everyone's," she says.

"Well, certainly not Cooper's. Is he going to survive this, Lyl?"

"Whether you've seen it or not, Cooper was never going to succeed. He wasn't going to capture David. He wasn't going to kill him either. Hector made a shit call when he offered this hit to Cooper, and that jackass was as good as dead the minute he decided to take the contract."

"We'll, we've certainly helped guarantee that."

The rumble of casters navigating brick cancels Lylian's rebuttal. Behind six carts, David's kitchen staff arrives wearing head-to-toe black. Three men and three women, one behind each of the roaming buffets. Stainless steel chafing dishes and domed serving trays, polished to a high shine, hide the meal that awaits, including its scent. As the staff pushes the carts around the table, Lylian and Casey turn to face the spectacle. They play the part of genuinely intrigued guests with eager appetites, and, in near unison, both wander closer to examine the feast.

The culinary team efficiently places each new salver upon the table, removing every lid without any regard for Casey and Lylian's approval. One loose aroma after another collides. The courses, delivered in no traditional order, create a soupy cloud of scent that is repulsive. When the carts' tops and lower shelves have no food left, the laborers manhandle the empty trollies away from the table. Without a word, they disappear into the hollows of the home.

"Casey, I don't want to fight with you. I love you, I do—"

"David and I might be fucking brothers, Lyl."

"I doubt that."

"No you don't," Casey says. "Look at me. Head to toe. Now add muscle, color, and sixty pounds—"

"Even if it's true, it wouldn't change how I feel about you."

"Just tell me you didn't know."

"I didn't... we don't, not for sure. This is David we're talking about."

"It doesn't matter, not right now. We have to think about Ruby. You have to do what you have to... to keep her safe. If that puts me in danger, so be it. Believe it or not, I've made peace with that."

"Have you seen this?" she asks as she waves her hand over the feast before them. "Have you seen any of this already?"

Casey sighs, "I don't think I needed to foresee anything here to know what David has in mind."

Involuntarily, Casey's eyes consume the rhyme-less spread. Categorizing and calculating calories, it's what he does.

"Eat to see, see to live," he mumbles.

"What did you say?"

"He's going to make me eat. He's going to ask me to read."

Lylian reaches for Casey's hand. He allows the connection.

"This feels different," she says, drawing Casey away from his estimations. "This feels final."

Casey breathes in the whole of the table, the food upon it and the chairs around it. He squeezes Lylian's fingers, "I'll admit, it is troubling that David is convening an audience to watch me do either of those things."

As if on cue, two of David's mercenaries arrive through an open gate at the rear of the courtyard. The vast desert behind them looks almost gentle, if not inviting. Heavily armed and in full fatigues, each man walks casually past Casey and Lylian. They take their seats across from one another and set their rifles in a lean against the table. Their pistols stay holstered at their sides.

"Tonight, the head of the table belongs to you, Casey!"

David's booming proclamation rings about the concrete ceiling of the arched canopy over their heads. The laugh on the coattails of his announcement precedes his physical entrance.

Casey and Lylian turn around to address him. Before

either can protest, David pulls out the chair at one head of the table. With a firm finger, he points down into the seat's availability.

"I insist," he emphasizes, "Please don't make me ask twice. We all know that I won't."

Casey lets go of Lylian's hand. He shuffles to his place, then sits. David leaves him there to sort out the rest of his preparations. Casey urges the chair closer to the table, slowly unfolds the napkin from his plate, and places it atop his lap.

Lylian chooses the chair nearest to her. David makes no objection. She will be well within his reach. He is all hyena smiles as he sits at the table's other end. With David so near and a soldier of some mass to Lylian's right, Casey may as well be just another star in the twilight sky.

The sixth chair remains empty. It is at David's left, full place setting at the ready. The staff had filled both its glasses along with the others. Casey can't take his eyes away from the unoccupied omen.

The servers return, pushing a portable spit that boasts the carcass of a whole pig, roasting over fire and stone.

"I hope you are hungry," David says. "I am absolutely famished."

Nearly every North American meat dish is represented on the table. Beef at all temperatures, stacked high, sits among an expected palette of vegetables in bowls. The remaining colors of the rainbow are there in the form of pies, cakes, and cookies. Cheese plates, breads, dressings, dips, and fried finger foods are scattered in the gaps between the larger courses.

As the cooks settle the spit, David reaches for his glass. He chooses the sparkling water that sits beside red wine. He raises it and waits for each of them to lift any glass of their own. They all oblige, but only Casey joins David in refraining from the booze at hand.

"It's just wonderful to have you both here," David says. Then, with hard eyes on Casey, he toasts. "To blood." He sips from his glass, but only his men follow suit.

On the heels of his toast, the resemblance hits even harder. Casey dwells in this new understanding of who David is, looks to Lylian for confirmation. Her eyes betray the denial she speaks as she stands.

"Enough with that crap already, David." she says. "This is bat-shit even for you."

David returns Lylian to her seat with a push.

What had been subtle, mostly due to the health about David's face, has grown more obvious. And there is no shaking that recognition now. David might as well be William, back from the dead. There is no trace of Virginia Anne about him, but every Banks' feature is plain to see.

"Our last guest is running late," David says. "I don't feel like waiting, do you? Let's dig in!"

The staff begins to serve the pig directly from the spit. Each slice slaps hard onto its plate, the thickest of which is plopped onto Casey's. He lets the meat float alone on his dish as he silently pulls at Lylian's attention, but she refuses to face him.

Casey turns to David, studies the man painfully. He watches as David piles his own helping high. He is unable to sit still, and his breathing sounds troubled.

David signals a server. The lackey grabs Casey's dish and loads it up with a little bit of everything else from the table. Casey looks down at the congregation, a slapdash heap held together by the squish of various gravies. The foods seek out their own territory upon his plate until they have little choice left but to marry themselves into one amorphous blob. It might as well be slop at this point, and its hugeness holds Casey in a trance until David speaks.

"The other day, I was thinking: The first time I so graciously housed you, I never made you witness the endings to the many lives that, ultimately, you were responsible for snuffing out."

He emphasizes the observation by stabbing his fork into the red raw of a steak filet. Shimmering scarlet juices pool out from underneath the slab. He dangles the filet on his fork in front of his face.

"Wasn't that kind of me?" He pushes the whole cut into his mouth and finishes the sentiment with no regard for the beef that crowds it. "Very brotherly, if you ask me."

The soldiers nod. Their agreement is immediate.

He finishes chewing, soaks the pink from around his mouth with his napkin, and holds his fork over a platter of Roasted Cornish Game Hen.

"I wonder though, Casey," David says, "do you have the stomach for the future that lies ahead?"

Two other soldiers emerge from the shadows settling in around the courtyard. They have Cooper by his arms and are dragging him to the table.

"I can assure you, it will be no accidental rifle shot like the one that killed William."

Lylian looks to David, then to Casey, and swallows a minor heave. She has the stir of about to be sick.

Before she can interject, the men prop Cooper's body on the last empty chair next to David. He is blindfolded and gagged with a white dishrag fastened with packing tape. They bind his arms behind his back. The rise and fall, then tilt and sway of his head is that of a man wrestling with the effects of heavy narcotics. His resistance to being detained in front of the dinner party is minimal. The men remove his blindfold and leave.

"I'm going to make this easy for you," David says. "I want you to read."

"For who?" Casey asks.

"For Cooper, of course."

"How far ahead?"

"That's the easiest part," David chuckles.

"How far, David?" Casey shouts, trying to impose some sense of control.

"Mm, let's say one half hour from now."

Cooper shakes his arms behind his back, rubbing the knot at his wrists into a spindle. The mumbles he makes behind his muzzle are panicked, but his quick hit of adrenaline is no match for the dope they have him on. His fight loses steam quick.

Casey throws his napkin atop the congealing mass on his plate. "I won't do it, David. I won't. I can't."

"Oh, I think you will."

Without warning, David thrusts his fork down with a tremendous force, shoving its prongs deep into Cooper's thigh. Through the gag, his scream is uniquely dull. The fit of broken coughs that follow the howl is that of a man choking on his own terror.

"I'm only asking you to try," David says.

He grabs Cooper at the back of his head, then throws his face through the plate and into the table. The dish crushes to pieces. He brings Cooper's face back up for display. Blood runs from his nose, soaks into the rag stuffed into his mouth, inflates it red the way water engorges a sponge.

Lylian looks away, but David snatches her face by the chin and drives her attention to the carnage.

"She's a wonderful actor, isn't she?" he shouts at Casey. "Pretending to be unfamiliar with my business, as if she hasn't seen it firsthand on multiple occasions."

"Fuck you," Lylian says.

He releases her and reaches for a sharp knife. He lays its tip into Cooper's right ear, then slowly begins to twirl it as he edges the point of the blade deeper into the canal.

Cooper's moan is no longer human.

Lylian looks at Casey. It didn't seem possible, but he's somehow gone paler.

"I swear I didn't know about this—about any of it," she says. "Honestly, I've no fucking idea what's going on."

The two soldiers keep eating, one even grabbing for a roll as the blood-sport unfolds in front of them.

"Read for Cooper, Casey, I'm practically begging you," David says, eyes wandering toward Lylian. "Or we'll move on to someone we actually care about."

David kicks Cooper's chair violently. It sends his whole body to the floor and the chair shatters beneath his weight. He sprawls atop the broken spindles, his arms freed. David reaches down for one of the chair's detached legs and stands as he finds it. He is a skyscraper over a body already in ruins. He points the splintered fangs of the leg's broken end at Cooper and demands, "Let's get to it, Casey. Time to eat!"

Casey sits back down. Without another word, he stabs his fork into the meat on his plate, the whole portion. He works the beef he's chewing to the back of his tongue to make more room. He stuffs his mouth with two handfuls of butter-soaked broccoli, then adds a ladle of black beans and sausage just as quickly. He swallows while biting into chocolate cake, then tears at breaded cutlets with his teeth. He searches the table for fat while still chewing. He pushes wedges of avocado into his mouth, a deviled egg, then vanilla pudding. He grabs a potato skin loaded with cheese and bacon, uses it like a cannon rammer, shoving at what's already in his mouth and clearing the way for more. Anything fried he grabs as fast as he can and slugs it down with the thick brown gravy from multiple boats.

For the first time, David's soldiers look authentically disturbed. Each man is resting their silverware on the table. Each man is squarely, if not immovably transfixed on Casey. All eyes are on him now, as he shoves, grinds, and crams every morsel at his end of the table into his mouth. He chews recklessly and swallows sadistically. There is no order to the insertions. There is no rationale to each new selection. The evidence of each last bite only exists at the sides of every additional cramming. All the colors of the table smear upon his face.

Lylian leaps from her seat, but David grabs her by her hair before she can make it to Casey.

"Whoa, whoa, whoa!" David finally shouts. "Don't fucking kill yourself, Casey. No one here wins if we let that happen."

There's the sudden pop of a pistol. A bullet rips through David's left leg, just above the kneecap. The impact casts him backward and he falls to the ground.

The solider closest to Cooper fumbles at his waist for his sidearm. It is no longer there. He only finds it when he looks to Cooper's outstretched and trembling hand.

Another shot rings out as Cooper puts everything he has into squeezing the trigger a second time. The second bullet misses. The nearest soldier is already in the air, his body comes crashing down upon Cooper's. He wrangles Cooper by the neck, compressing his throat between his bicep and wrist. The other man swings himself over the table like he medaled in pommel horse, lands his boots into the fat of Cooper's forearm. The gun drops from Cooper's hand and the men secure his limbs under their knees.

Cooper manages a weak but victorious laugh.

"God dammit!" David shouts. He reaches for the top rail of his chair, pulls himself up from the floor. Using the seat like a crutch, he ambles closer to Cooper. "I mean, God dammit! That was some real, live cowboy shit, right there. And I don't impress easy."

The soldiers manage to quarter Cooper's body flat on the ground for David. One holds Cooper's arms, the other has him by the feet.

"Hang onto him tight now," David says to his men. "Don't you even think about letten 'im go."

With his good leg, he crushes his boot into Cooper's head, over and over again. His men hold the body tight, though its thrash is short-lived. David is fifteen stomps in when the crack of bone gives way to indecipherable reverberations. Nothing remains to fracture, break, or even identify, and David stops.

He falls back into his chair, then stares at Cooper's corpse. His eyes still wide, alive in admiration for the man's valiant last stand.

The soldiers look at one another, less impressed and more disgusted, assessing how best to deal with the remains on the floor between them. A mess that is surely theirs to clean.

David grabs for some napkins from the table while evaluating his wound. He looks up to see that Casey and Lylian's chairs are empty.

"Well, Plan B, I guess," he says to himself.

He fashions the cloths into a tourniquet, ties it tight around his leg, stands, then limps to the courtyard's rear gate. He looks out across the darkening landscape, scanning it until he lands on two shadows on the run. He shows no signs of urgency and stops his men when they look as if they might immediately go after Casey and Lylian.

"Not yet," he says. "Let's give those two a head start. After all, they're family."

Subject: CASEY BANKS
Interviewer: [redacted]
Date of Interview: 12/23/2015
CB=Casey Banks, IN=Interviewer

IN: This interview is being recorded. The time is 12:03PM. Let's get started, shall we?

CB: No good afternoon, no how are you today, [redacted]?

IN: Good afternoon, Casey. How are you?

CB: I'm doing well, thank you. How are you?

IN: To be honest, I'm disappointed.

CB: Disappointed about what?

IN: Disappointed with you, unfortunately.

CB: I've been a model subject for months. If I've let you down, perhaps you and the team set the bar too high.

IN: It wouldn't hurt for you to aim higher.

CB: Okay, what did or didn't I do?

IN: You haven't been entirely honest with me.

CB: If there have been inconsistencies, present them to me. I am more than happy to set the record straight on any information I have given you.

IN: You read for the team yesterday.

CB: I did.

IN: Were you able to activate a vision?

CB: Have you bothered to watch the recording?

IN: I did. You seemed off, to be honest. So, I'm asking, were you able to activate a vision?

CB: Off?

IN: Don't act like you don't know what I'm talking about.

CB: It is *your* accusation. Enlighten me.

IN: When they are legitimate, your visions are very detailed. Excruciatingly so. Beyond the actions taking place, it's like your brain can't help but see and report every detail.

CB: You are suggesting I made it up? Because what, my descriptions didn't have enough color?

IN: I think you did your best to mimic the way you report what you see from someone's timeline when the vision is real.

CB: Maybe you have simply become used to the way I deliver that information. I think you should watch the video again.

IN: I watched yesterday's twice and reviewed others. The differences are subtle, but they're there.

CB: Well, I don't know what you want me to tell you.

IN: Tell me the truth.

CB: I have always told you as much as I can.

IN: The team told me you chose the target destination for yesterday's reading.

CB: I made a suggestion.

IN: For yesterday's subject you chose two months from now.

CB: Two months from yesterday, to be precise. After all, we don't want to fuck up the details, do we?

IN: That future date is the furthest into a timeline you have attempted with us.

CB: The team seemed pretty excited to acquire data related to a reading that deep.

IN: I'm sure they were.

CB: So, what's the problem?

IN: I'm guessing you won't be around two months from now when they realize that what you have reported won't come to pass.

CB: My time here has never been a forever thing.

IN: I know you purged your reading meal last night. After the session, after you left the reading room.

CB: I thought you said there were no cameras in my room.

IN: There aren't.

CB: Ah, are there odors hanging around in the room, then?

IN: You thought a later start to today's interview might give the smell time to dissipate?

CB: No. I wanted to run this morning. I thought maybe you were smelling the byproducts of that workout. I mean, the treadmill is right fucking there.

IN: Vomit and sweat are two entirely different smells. All I smell is soap. Soap and bullshit.

CB: What your point, [redacted]?

IN: Are you done reading for us, Casey?

CB: The reading I did for the team one week ago, what I reported, didn't it come to pass?

IN: That vision was accurate, yes. But you didn't throw-up after performing that reading. And, as you had stated, you didn't throw up the entire time I was on holiday. I'll admit, I was impressed. In fact, until last night, you hadn't purged in several weeks. I believed you were making real progress here with—

CB: Lylian told you I purged the meal.

IN: She did. Does that surprise you?

CB: We all have different agendas here, so, no. It doesn't make it any less of a bummer to hear though.

IN: Lylian is concerned. She is looking out for your wellbeing. Her chief motivation is probably Ruby's wellbeing, but isn't your own health an important piece to that?

CB: I'm guessing she told you that during your extended absence I was performing my own readings.

IN: Let's pretend I know nothing.

CB: Okay then, [redacted]. I was doing readings that whole time. Are we square?

IN: If I may, I'd like to address the elephant in the room.

CB: Go for it.

IN: At some point, you must have realized that evacuating meals was inhibiting your ability to see. To be more specific, you must have realized that even thinking about purging right after a reading was having a detrimental effect on your ability to activate a vision.

CB: Hasn't that been your theory all along?

IN: It was *a* theory. But I think you've known it was true for some time. Or at least had speculated as much.

CB: Speculations are futile. I didn't know, until I knew. And honestly, I believe there is a balance to the whole thing that can still be achieved.

IN: Not with us.

CB: I beg your pardon?

IN: I'm not saying you won't crack it, Casey. There are many variables. How much you eat, how far you wish to travel forward, how long you wait after a reading to evacuate what's left of the meal. What you weigh when the reading starts. The list goes on and on. It's possible you'll have good readings and bad, accurate then non-existent. And that may be fine for a guy who just wants to make more cash, but it sounds risky to me. It doesn't matter though, it's not what we're asking you to do here, and—

CB: In my def—

IN: Let me finish, please. God knows I've let you ramble.

CB: By all means, finish telling me how this plays out.

IN: The team has no interest in encouraging you to continue practicing any activity we believe will kill you.

CB: So, anorexia is A-OK, but you guys draw the line at bulimia?

IN: Not exactly. At first, yes—

CB: Thumbs up to anorexia, everyone!

IN: But we'd be interested in working with you to find a healthier path forward. A beneficial one too.

CB: And what does that look like?

IN: Have you ever stopped to consider you might be able to see just by eating a lot? By occasionally eating too much, like a regular person might eat from time to time?

CB: Oh, I see.

IN: What?

CB: Your team wants the gift, but none of the gift's baggage.

IN: Don't you want the same?

CB: I'm accustomed to the mess.

IN: Sure. Sometimes there is comfort in discomfort. I understand your situation. It's—

CB: Not as well as I understand your situation.

IN: This back and forth no longer seems constructive.

CB: What are you hoping for here?

IN: Imagine what you could do for yourself, and for the world, if you read just once a month. Imagine how deep you might travel if you allowed a gargantuan meal to simply be. What are the possibilities of a guy who can see the future, when that guy is also interested in living healthier so he can live longer? What are the possibilities if you were to finally become comfortable in your own skin?

CB: I hate to break it to you, [redacted], but I've read ahead. Countless times, in fact. And the ending is always the same.

9

He is running for his life.

Casey and Lylian sprint away from the compound, away from the dinner, and away from Cooper's slaughter.

Their attempt at an escape feels familiar. Maybe any run made by a man who runs habitually ends up giving that impression.

Even barefoot, Casey's lope is animal. He is a marred jack rabbit, tearing around the track's native hurdles, zigzagging around the natural landmines that emerge from the hardpacked desert floor. Tints of green at the tips of skeletal scrub seemingly bend at his will. But tiny bright pops of color in front of each consecutive step threaten to upend him. The miniature flowers are a ruse. They are like kaleidoscopic hairbows worn to disguise the brutality of thorns and needles on the heads of the cacti that call this stretch home.

In the final minutes of a setting sun, all the damning evidence of the local floras' indifference to Casey's plight is easy to see. The evidence is wet red. Active pinpricks and gashes, opened along heel to toe, have patterned his pants' cuffs in a speckle of blood.

It hasn't slowed Casey down. A good guess would be a four-minute and fifteen-second mile. He should be focused on his survival, but his *how fast am I going* estimations are obvious. Calories burn. Calculating the totals he sheds, even while trying to stay alive, is a given. Old habits die hard. In this case, his habit of wanting to know what his body stands to lose for his exertion may just go to the grave with him.

Save for the dull, frenzied patter of their own four feet, and puffs of hard breaths, the desert is predictably silent. The two of them exchange nothing. The run takes everything. They are free, but the lead they hold is illusionary at best.

There are moments where Casey could pass for the wind. If Lylian wasn't in tow, he might be able to create a lead that mattered. He cranes his head backward to find her and winces before he can pinpoint her location. He doesn't have to look at his feet to know they have been compromised. Tiny darkening pools of blood are left in the compressed and rust-colored silt of each step. He absorbs the pain, resigning himself to it. When he finds the red blur of Lylian's dress, he seems satisfied with her effort. Even so, he slows to keep the distance between them from growing any larger.

Ahead of them lies the promise of nothing. It is a disheartening repetition. Open mile after open mile of dirt, rock, and scattered hazards. Any cactus taller than a toddler casts a long, strange shadow. Soon those shadows will give way to the mountain's own. When the sun has finished its descent, twilight might allow for twenty-or-so minutes more of actual running. Thereafter, the darkness of the desert might provide the two of them some cover, but the same darkness that *might* hide them won't be as kind if they keep running. People don't often think desert when they hear the words "mountain lion."

A quarter-mile behind them, bright headlights appear. Eight beams bumbling in chase, popping in and out of sight as they navigate the desert's knolls. There's at least two men standing in the bed of each truck, clinging to roll bars behind the cabs. They have night vision goggles slung around their necks. The low bark of their orders rides the wind, and every truck has artillery mounted to it.

It doesn't take long for the tinny buzz of a drone to join the search party. The airborne spy catches up to Casey fast. He tries to shake it by zigging left, zagging right, but the drone adjusts with no problem. No matter his pace or direction, the technology easily matches it. The trucks have halved the distance already, and the lead vehicle quickly sets its direction on Casey and Lylian.

His body's preparations for vomit blanch his face, but Casey can't make sick on the run. He's tried in the past. He races up the slant of a large, scorched rock flat, then comes to a stop. His inhalations sound thin and his eyes strain to take stock of the terrain ahead. As the sun's crown sinks, the hellscape revamps into a seductive dream. Purple and blue hues are the day's last act. Any ditches, deep or shallow, have been erased by the two-dimensional effect of semidarkness. There are no twinkling lights in any direction, no indications of reachable towns, no smoke from pueblos, or last sounds of ranching machinery winding down.

Casey doesn't look back for Lylian. The cholla cacti and brush around him are illuminated by the high beams approaching behind him. This is the finish line. The race is over.

Casey's fingers instinctively go into his mouth. His index and middle find their way in, down, and hard against his gag reflex. When he pulls his fist from his throat, a discordant mess ejects, splattering across the dirt in a wet rhythm. He bends at the waist, loses himself in the ecstasy of his heaves. It's a brief victory, the glint in his eyes is fleeting. He raises the same combination of fingers to his mouth, but doesn't commit to another jab. He is done. He drops his hands to his knees, then looks down at the puddle of foul mishmash just in front of his bruised and bleeding feet. Once vibrant colors are now pale. There are a few distinct flecks of blood on clumps of meat gone pearly from digestion.

Casey sways as his eyes try to close. He steadies himself long enough to turn around. The headlamps are blinding. With one hand over his brow, he searches for Lylian. Her black form is fast approaching against the backlight of the vehicles racing toward them. She waves at Casey wildly, as if she were a lost then found friend at an outdoor music festival. It is a sweet moment, a brief mirage of normalcy created by the inadvertently comical motion of her limbs going amok.

She is some fifty yards out when nausea gets the best of him. He falls backward and hits the ground with a thick squish.

Lylian pushes herself into a marathoner's final sprint.

At the top of the rock, she finds Casey lying in the puddle of vomit. The crisscrossing high beams and the reverberating roar of engines gives their reunion a strange disco vibe. It's not that exactly. It feels like a rescue scene dramatization, made with cheap strobe lights as part of some off-off-off-Broadway play. She kneels at his side. The bottoms of her feet are shredded and her breathing is hard and fast. With the precision of a child playing doctor, she runs her fingers along his wrists and then up to his neck. She pushes the tips deep to find a pulse, then brings her mouth to his ear as her lungs collect enough oxygen to form a whisper.

"Don't you fucking die on me. I need you. Ruby needs you."

There is no response.

Crack.

The first slap to his face lands weakly.

"Come on, Casey, wake up."

Crack! The second hit has more velocity.

"Wake up, God Dammit."

Crack! Crack! Crack! One after another, each grows in strength.

Casey doesn't stir. She fights to hold back tears, but the dust on her face is streaked by the few that managed to escape.

There is the smell of vomit, and then, the faintest scent of Lylian's perfume. Woodsy notes foreign to the West Texas desert, and a hint of jasmine, pepper, and clove. The fragrance tries to assert itself, meandering its way through the airborne molecules of the half-digested foods and gastric juices soaking into his trousers.

The drone above shoots off toward the compound as the truck's lights converge upon them. She slaps more, she slaps harder. The repetition achieves nothing. She stands, puts one hand to her nose, then, using the other, she drags Casey's body from out of the puddle. The ease of which she is able to move him onto drier ground is concerning. When his body is settled, she drops to his side again. No more slaps, just an intense focus on catching her breath.

It is quite unnecessary, but there is a truck on each side of the rock now. Doors open, and boots drop to the ground, connecting themselves to the earth, almost in unison.

There will be no escape.

Lylian stands to be seen.

"Aquí arriba, idiotas! Come help me with him already."

IN: This interview is being recorded. The time is 9:45AM. Happy new year, Casey.

CB: We're leaving.

IN: I was afraid the Christmas break might have that effect.

CB: On the contrary, the break was fine.

IN: I'm glad to hear that. What did you and Lylian get up to?

CB: All I can say is thank God for on-demand.

IN: Leaving this facility is what Lylian wants?

CB: It took some convincing, I made a few concessions. But ultimately, our next steps were made mutually.

IN: Concessions?

CB: Agreements pertaining to my health.

IN: Lylian wants you to seek some form of treatment?

CB: I imagine she does, but for now she will just have to take my word for it when I say my eating disorders won't be her problem forever.

IN: What promises have you made?

CB: To her? None. No addiction is beaten that way, you know that, I'm certain.

IN: Any to yourself, then?

CB: One.

IN: Care to share it with me?

CB: I want to live out my days as the best version of myself.

IN: And that journey can't continue here?

CB: This isn't the real world. If anything, it is a distraction *from* the real world.

IN: We'll have to agree to disagree on that, I'm afraid.

CB: Will you worry about me?

IN: Of course, I will. But I adhere to a pretty stringent set of personal boundaries. It's an exercise of the mind, and not always a picnic. I'm not saying I'm better at keeping a necessary distance from my patients than other therapists, but I do pride myself on it.

CB: You work hard at not caring, then?

IN: Over the years, I've had several patients opt out of treatment with me far too early in the process. And I worried about them all, but I can't dwell on each and every one. If they don't come back to see me, I can only hope they find the help they need with someone else.

CB: Would you want to see me again?

IN: I'd rather you just stay here, and put in the necessary work now. And you know that.

CB: But if we were to bump into each other, down the road, outside of your professional trappings, would it make you happy?

IN: That depends.

CB: On what?

IN: Are you healthy when this happens?

CB: Maybe.

IN: Well, if we do meet again, that'd be my preference.

CB: Do you know who you work for, [redacted]?

IN: I work for myself, Casey. If you are asking me if I know what entity pays me to be a part of this study, the answer is yes.

CB: Are you certain of that?

IN: It's right there on the paystub. They aren't handing me brief-cases stuffed with cash under a table in a dimly lit backroom.

CB: (inaudible)

IN: That I'm making money to treat you continues to rub you the wrong way. Is that why you are leaving?

CB: No.

IN: If I were to stay on, gratis, would you consider staying, too?

CB: Would you actually do that?

IN: Would it make a difference?

CB: It just did. But I'm afraid we are still leaving.

IN: Where will you two go?

CB: I don't think it is wise for me to outline our itinerary.

IN: It's not like I'm going to follow you, Casey.

CB: Nonetheless.

IN: When you are back on the outside, are you hoping to reunite with Cooper?

CB: Not if we can help it, no.

IN: Don't you think he'll be looking for you?

CB: That seems likely.

IN: God, Casey. Cut the bullshit. You've seen a timeline in which Cooper finds you, haven't you?

CB: At this point, I no longer think it is beneficial for me to share anything I have seen with you or the team.

IN: Will you be reading out there?

CB: If it helps me and Lylian, yes.

IN: And she's okay with that?

CB: I think she is agreeable to anything that aids in creating a new chapter for her and Ruby. And I have no intention of over-doing it. If I do read, I won't push it. I promise. We'll follow the rules that worked before. Once upon a time, I had this power under control, and there's no reason to believe I can't capture control of the whole situation again.

IN: Well, I wish you luck.

CB: That's it?

IN: What else do you want me to say, Casey? Should I beg you to use the money you inherited to better your chances at any kind of second life? Away from David? Should I beat the dead horse in the room, scream over and over again that I think both you and Lylian's best interests are better served if, and only if, you continue on here?

CB: No, you should not.

IN: I've made these points. I've made them all clearly. And it has become painfully obvious, at least to me, that nothing I've said —nothing I could say—is going to change your mind about remaining a part of this program. So, yes. I wish you luck. And I mean it.

CB: I didn't mean to upset you.

IN: Don't apologize. It's okay. I shouldn't have let my emotions get the better of me.

CB: Can I make a small observation?

IN: Sure.

CB: I don't think you realize how much you've already helped me, [redacted].

IN: No offense, Casey, but plenty of patients have said those very same words on their way out the door to a full-blown relapse. It's of no comfort, I'm sorry.

CB: I don't doubt that. But I'm not about to let the weak willpower of a handful of strangers invalidate my sincerity. The day I made the decision to meet you was the right one. My time here has been well spent.

IN: The day *you* made the decision?

CB: You know what I mean.

IN: (inaudible)

CB: What's funny?

IN: I honestly thought today was going to be a bit more routine. That sounded awful. What I mean to say is, I arrived today, eager to hear more of your history. Or at least to hear more of your side of that story, anyway.

CB: My side of what story?

IN: The early days of your being able to see. The months before Lylian killed Diego, when reading was working out for you two. The time you spent falling in love with Lylian. All of it.

CB: Whose side have you heard?

IN: Lylian's, of course.

CB: You have been interviewing Lylian?

IN: She never told you?

CB: I am sure whatever Lylian told you is accurate enough.

IN: Oh, I'm sure too.

CB: So, what now?

IN: Is one last question too much to ask?

CB: I think I have the time.

IN: What are you really running from, do you think?

CB: A better question would be, what am I running toward.

IN: And?

CB: Is *my destiny* a dumb answer?

IN: Coming from you, I'm not sure any other answer would do.

CB: This time, that's a compliment, right?

IN: I guess it's whatever you want it to be.

CB: (inaudible)

IN: If you ever decide you want to get better, I want you to reach out to me.

CB: Your optimism kills me.

IN: Hard to do what I do without being eternally so.

CB: I can imagine.

IN: The groups I told you about, will you consider them?

CB: When and if there is time.

IN: That's all I can ask. I don't say this to all of my patients, Casey, but I do believe I'll see you again, at some point.

CB: Not if I see you first, [redacted].

10

He is well.

Atop a pink four-poster bed, Casey sleeps. Under his light blue johnny gown, the shape of his body is subtly plump. Warm hues paint his cheeks and lips. The tubes and wires link him to various machines. He is breathing on his own. Proteins, carbohydrates, fats, vitamins and minerals are delivered where they belong. The ticks and pings of the medical devices surrounding the bed are steady, rhythmic, calming. Pulse, body temperature, respiration rate, blood pressure: all the measurements are a lot closer to normal.

The rest of the bedroom's décor is mostly mauve on other mauves. Its regular inhabitant's possessions are in stark contrast to the sickbed set-up pulsing among them. It's a child's hideaway, one that hasn't yet given up on its youthful innocence, though there are tokens of recent angst. Store-bought rebellion, indications of a young girl's move toward a young woman's independence dot the room. The teen she aspires to be can be gleaned from the handful of darker novelties tucked about floating shelves. In time, their mood will own the place, pushing out all traces of childish things. But until then, "Live Your

Dream!" rules the room, shouting non-stop from a poster hanging just above Casey's head.

Lylian sleeps at the foot of his impromptu gurney, her legs hung over one side of the fuzzy pink papasan chair.

Casey comes to.

He shakes his haze and looks around the room. From high and low, dozens of stuffed animals stare back at him. Pinned to a corkboard on the wall across from his bed are the smiles of children, it is not an observation he is able to blink away. This is not a dream.

He rolls his gaze over the footboard where he discovers Lylian. He pauses, eyes frozen on her as if trying to decide whether to call out to her or leave her asleep. Her hair is styled and her tan skin has darkened. Even from his bed, she smells like long walks. He lets her alone and continues evaluating his situation.

On the wooden table to his right, he finds a small army of nutritional supplements. Their labels seem comically mature next to the digital cube clock wrapped in the candy colors of unicorn print. The squared numbers, digits floating against a fuchsia LED display, flit from 4:48PM to 4:49PM, to 4:50PM. Casey breaks from the clock. He reaches for a bottle marked "potassium," and becomes acutely aware of the dangling cables plugged into his arms and torso.

Mobility doesn't come quick. He sits up, panic in the tremble of each moving limb. The devices monitoring his vitals jump as he works through his fear. He runs a hand over the electrodes taped to his chest, then reaches for the tube and catheter sticking out of his left arm. He leaves the intravenous line just as quickly to start yanking at the feeding tube running into his stomach.

"Casey, rip that shit out if you want," Lylian says. "But I don't know what half of these machines are up to, and I doubt you'll want to find out."

She stands and approaches him cautiously, but her movement wilts Casey deep into his bed. His beat-dog reaction stops her. She withdraws a hand that had been moving toward his knee and takes a small step back.

"Believe it or not, this is already the longest you've been alert."

He takes another look at his body. A turtle set for dissection.

"What the fuck, Lyl?"

His voice is loud, raw from days of neglect.

She shushes him with a finger, then turns her head to the closed door. It is quiet. She drops her request for silence and leans over Casey, continuing in a whisper, "We aren't alone here."

"Where *is* here, Lylian?" Casey asks. He has made a noticeable new commitment to secrecy. "Whose room is this?"

"Right now, all that matters is you are alive."

"Answer my question," Casey says. He works his torso into a posture resembling seated, then threatens within his hush, "Tell me, Lyl, or I swear to God, I'll fucking rip everything out of me right now."

He grips the feeding tube to show that he means business, but Lylian ignores the ultimatum. She cups her hand to his face and he swats the gesture away, with more force than he'd intended. In doing so, he nearly falls to the floor and the IV separates from the cannula taped in the back of his hand. Lylian reaches for his shoulders, grabbing both in time to keep him from tumbling off the bed. She steadies him, pushing his body into the pillows. He works to free himself, but even in new health, he is no match for her vigor. When he is still, she leans over his body, takes his hand, and gently reinserts the IV.

"If you give me some time, I can better this situation. Our situation." The volume she had previously insisted upon is no more. She tucks a third pillow behind his back and says, "Until I can sort it out, you are just going to have to accommodate David."

The rhythm of the monitors slows in parallel to his body's surrender.

"I'm not going to read for him," he says.

"Not forever, no."

"No, Lyl. Not ever."

The bedroom door swings open, slapping against a spring doorstopper.

"How can you be so certain, Casey?" David asks.

He doesn't wait for Lylian and Casey to decouple. He moseys into the room, smug, even on his brand-new limp. He takes a quick look at the time on his watch, looks up at them both, and fakes a repulsed squirm.

"You'd think by now I'd be used to you two being a thing. I am decidedly not, but I promise to keep working at it."

Lylian nudges Casey into the pillows at his back, just enough to sit him tight. She turns and sets herself as an obstacle. David humors her. He stops, bristling just for show.

"You said I had some time to talk to Casey alone," she says. "About next steps."

"That time has passed. You should have woken him sooner."

Lylian holds her ground. Behind her, Casey surveils the room again. If he is looking for impromptu weapons to wield, there is little to be found that doesn't come with puffs, glitter, or anything more than a fictional threat.

"I'm going to have to ask you to sit, Lylian. Or, I can make you sit," David says. "The choice, as always, is yours."

She doesn't budge.

"Give me five more minutes, please," she says.

David is indifferent to her saccharine tone.

"There isn't five more minutes. Now sit the fuck down!"

She remains an obstacle. Readies herself.

David's balled fist goes to half-cocked in the air.

"It's fine, Lylian! It's fine. Just sit down, I'll be fine," Casey interrupts.

David holds the moment hostage with his hovering warning.

"Lyl, please sit. I'm fine," Casey repeats.

She shuffles aside, then plunks back down upon the pink papasan.

David lowers his fist and finishes his slow stroll toward Casey. He stops when he reaches a spot between the bed and the room's only window.

"You must be wondering where we are, Big Brother."

"We are not related, you fucking psycho."

The insult brings a smile to David's face. He looks at his watch again. The minute hand shifts as if on cue, settling in on precisely twenty after five.

"If you can, Casey, I'd like for you to come look out this window with me."

Lylian starts to lift herself, "let me help him."

"No, no. He's a big boy, he's had his rest," David says. "You feel great, am I right?"

"I'm good, Lyl."

She sits back into her chair and David gives Casey the space to join him at the window.

He swings his legs over the side of the bed carefully. Even so, the machines seem unsteady. David snatches the swaying tubes in one hand to assist. The distance to the window isn't much, but David gently pulls at the IV's pole, rolling it closer to create the slack Casey needs.

"Can't have you fucking up the floors," David says, obliterating the authenticity of the kindness. "Come along."

David pulls the sheer curtain all the way to one side. When he can't find a place to catch the veil, he rips the fabric from its rod and casts the ruffled nuisance to the floor. He lays the full length and weight of his arm over Casey's shoulders, as if the two were affectionately inseparable pals taking in a mountain-top sunset.

Outside the pane lies an upscale neighborhood. The home's lots are large, each no less than an acre. All the houses are in a long, uniformed row, tucked to the rear of their parcels at roughly the same depth. The dwellings exist, uninspired, upon green grass that is only achievable when one has little regard for water scarcity. No two structures are the same, and yet every one of them has been built to specifications outlined by an unyielding association's by-laws. Their façades have been fashioned in the same stone, and the same amount of that stone, around four or five thousand square feet of living space. The handful of sedans and sport utility vehicles that are home for the evening are resting on long stained-and-sealed concrete driveways. Each car is a different model of the same rolling badge of wealth.

Casey steadies himself under the oppression of David's arm. He continues to stare outside, but doesn't keep his attention on any one detail.

"Where are we exactly?"

David looks to Lylian as if only she holds that information, but replies with an answer just the same.

"I believe we are staying at the Johnson's, right?"

Lylian confirms David's feigned guess with a half-hearted, but agreeable nod.

"Yes, the Johnson's," David repeats. "Good people. Lawyers maybe. Doctors. Lawyers and doctors is a good guess out here."

Casey's face goes frustratingly pained. "And did you kill the Johnsons?"

David's laugh shakes the walls. He joggles Casey's body between both his hands as if Casey were in on the joke.

"Of course not," he says while trying to control the after-shocks of his roar. "Seriously, Casey? I'm not a monster. We all have our rules. You definitely have yours."

Casey is visibly agitated, but he does not respond.

"Though Mister and Missus Johnson were not looking to make their home a vacation rental, they were more than happy to rent it to us. I made them a very nice cash offer, of course." David looks around the room, landing his thin ruminations at the hospital gadgets. "We rented the whole home *mostly* as is."

Casey looks to Lylian. She gives no indication that what David has said is untrue. David seems to sense Casey's reluctance to take him at his word.

"Long before I met you, before I had access to your powers, I always found it quite possible for one to do just about anything he wants to do in this world," David says. "*If* he truly wants to do it. But I won't deny that having vast sums of money can be very persuasive."

Casey's body tightens. "I'm sure there's a good reason, but why have you hospitalized me at The Johnson's?"

David doesn't offer any more details. He checks his watch again, the time is 5:25PM. His next words leave him feverishly. "I can understand your confusion, Casey. And I look forward to the fascinating chats we are sure to have, but, right now, I need you to pay close attention to what's outside. Look out the window, please."

Casey rests his eyes on David, refuses to turn toward the window again.

David's hand shifts from over Casey's shoulder and forms a vise on the back of his neck. "Please," he says again.

Casey obeys.

Other than the chirps of the electrocardiogram, the room is quiet.

Out the window, a brown Volvo rolls into view from underneath the canopy of aged trees down the road. The right blinker flashes and the car slows. There is a woman behind the wheel. Her blonde hair is pulled back tight, her ponytail only evident as she turns the station wagon into the driveway of the home across from them.

David can't contain his smirk.

"You aren't nearsighted, are you?" he asks.

Casey squints as the driver door opens. Before she exits, the woman inside grabs for a few colored folders and an oversized handbag from the passenger seat. She exits the car, lifting herself from the carriage while engaged in a call and shuffling her effects. She puts the back of her heeled foot into the door to close it. The conversation she is having is animated, but nothing is audible.

David practically dances in impatience. "Recognize her?"

"Candace," Casey soberly slips. He presses his forehead into the glass pane, instantly defeated.

"Candace," David repeats victoriously. "Or Doctor Ford, if we want to be a bit more formal."

Casey steps back from the window. He looks to Lylian. "I don't understand," he says. She has trouble meeting his stare.

"Oh, I think you get it," David assures him, pulling Casey back to the matter outside. "I don't think she can see us, but if you wanted, you could wave real big at her."

As Candace makes her way from the car to the front porch, the home's oversized entry opens. Two children, one boy and one girl, roughly the same age, come out racing. They go bounding down the stone steps, angling their point of attack directly at their mother. They sprint toward her with no regard for the dormant daylilies asleep in their garden beds. Candace ends her call as the tow-headed beasts reach her. Each is now a near-immovable object, tightly clamped to the Frankenstein-amble she works to carry them both with her into their home.

"How did you find her?" Casey asks.

"It wasn't hard," David says. "I have access to the addresses of every single person I have ever employed."

The recent addition of color in Casey's face vanishes. David lifts his arm from Casey's shoulder, allowing him to leave the window, offering him the space he needs to work out his agony.

"Casey—" Lylian starts, but David puts his hand up to stop whatever it is she is about to offer. She obliges and her eyes search the room for anything that isn't Casey's growing grief.

From a pained posture over the bed, Casey asks, "Did Candace know she was working for you?"

"No," David answers. "Her checks weren't signed by me personally. Huge checks by the way. She wasn't cheap."

Casey looks at Lylian. "You knew all along, didn't you?"

Tears slip down her checks, each riding the tail of the last.

"And if you knew that, then this whole time with me has been bullshit," Casey says. His anguish translates to a new ruckus of electrified beeps coming from the monitor. He rips the drip line from his hand and then the electrodes from his chest. Lylian steadies herself, but before he can land a second step, David collars him, then easily casts Casey back to the bed.

"Calm yourselves, both of you," David insists. "For what it's worth, Lylian had no idea. No clue about any of it. Not about the facility, and certainly not about my initial interest in finally meeting the man who killed my father."

Casey swings at David from the bed, but he misses horribly. David doesn't. A blow to the gut. It's enough to keep Casey still.

"What were the chances, right?" David asks, looking to Casey then to Lylian and then back to him. "Real small world shit, if you ask me."

Casey can't bring himself to look at either of them, so David grabs him at the back of his neck and forces him to look at Lylian.

"Imagine how surprised I was when what she'd told me about your ability to see the future turned out to be true. Quite the bonus!" he says. He starts a laugh but collects his poise quick. "I think she actually loves you though, as disgusting as that may be."

"I find that hard to believe," Casey says.

David doesn't respond. He's looking at the floor. The feeding tube attached to Casey's abdomen has come free. The open end of it lies on the oak hardwoods, its oatmeal-colored mixture calmly oozing into a small puddle there at David's feet. Its spread is enough to cause David to wince.

He steps back and asks, "You find which part hard to believe?"

"All of it."

"Introducing myself to you, Casey, that was always going to happen. At some point, anyway. But Lylian finding you first, that was just, well... fate, I guess."

"I do love you," Lylian tries in a broken sob. "I swear it."

"We all have a lot to catch-up on, and there will be plenty of time for that, but right now you have a pretty big decision in front of you," David says to Casey.

"And what's that?"

David pops him with the back of his hand. "Don't play dumb. How will the world know you, Big Brother? As just another traumatized plebe, or as the powerful man you can be? A powerful man who works for me, of course."

"And if I don't agree to read for you?"

"I'll torture and kill Candace." His answer is sharp and to the point. "And her husband. And then her children. And then, I don't know... her mother, if she's still alive. I think that's pretty obvious. It won't be the first time you and I kill someone who works for me either. Your best bet here is to keep reading for me." David returns to the window, looks outside, but turns back just as quickly. "No puking either. I know you love it, but it's not working. The research proves it, and you know it."

Now that David's offer has been said aloud and in detail, Casey's fight is gone, what little was left of it anyway. David scowls at the deflation of his spirt, he seems truly disappointed in Casey's reaction to the arrangement he has proposed.

"Think of it! You and me—you reading, and me doing whatever the fuck is necessary based on the visions you have. Together like we always should have been... had Dad not been so very concerned about appearances. So William knocked up his mistress, who the fuck hasn't?"

Casey rubs his face with both hands, then looks at Lylian who has run out of tears.

"Her name is Pamela, if you even give a damn," David adds.

"I don't," Casey says.

"Fair enough, though Mom *is* eager to meet you."

"What about Lylian," Casey asks, "what about Ruby?"

"I'm sure we can figure something out."

Casey is unsold.

Lylian less so.

"How will the world know us, Casey? Don't worry, I'm gonna tell ya. Together, we'll be unstoppable. William, God rest his soul, would be so fucking proud."

Subject: LYLIAN AYER
Interviewer: [redacted]
Date of Interview: 10/23/2015
LA=Lylian Ayer, IN=Interviewer

IN: This interview with Lylian Ayer is being recorded. The time is 2:30PM. Good afternoon, Lylian.

LA: Hi.

IN: Thank you for agreeing to this interview. As part of our research into Casey's condition, we are hoping to have semi-regular conversations with you, and with Casey. I had my first conversation with him this morning, but may not always meet with you on the same days I talk with him. And, as I understand it, you are under no obligation to meet with me during your and Casey's stay here. These interviews will typically start with questions around subjects the team gives me, but I'd like for them to be an open dialog. Honest answers will serve the mission here best. And, if you have questions, I'll also answer them truthfully.

LA: Can I ask one now?

IN: Of course.

LA: What is it you do, exactly? Professional interrogator?

IN: Right. I'm sorry. I wasn't made aware of just how up-to-speed either of you are. This whole thing has been a little shotgun, if I'm being honest. My name is [redacted], and I am a board-certified psychiatrist who specializes in treating patients suffering from eating disorders.

LA: Good luck with that.

IN: Guiding someone through recovery is never easy. There are successes and there are setbacks. One thing I do know for sure, a cynical attitude never helps.

LA: You don't know Casey.

IN: No, I don't. I'm eager to learn more about him though. And about you. Above all, I'm here to help.

LA: To "help?"

IN: Yes. Why are you here?

LA: I wouldn't know where to start.

IN: Does a reason for being at this facility with Casey need a beginning? Why are you here, Lylian? Why did you come with him?

LA: Is that unusual?

IN: How do you mean?

LA: You are acting like I know what this place even is. A safe-house? Some sort of secret recovery center? I doubt significant others are typically allowed to check-in with the patients.

IN: Do you believe Casey needs help?

LA: Jesus Christ, lady. You really are in the dark here.

IN: I'm aware the situation is unique. To be specific, I'm asking if you believe Casey needs help with his eating disorders.

LA: If you are looking for him to read here, you sure as hell aren't going to be able to address his eating disorders.

IN: Fair enough. So, I'll ask one more time, why are *you* here?

LA: You keep asking as if you believe I had a choice.

IN: Even if you didn't have a choice before, when I was briefed this morning, I was told you can leave this facility at any time. Without Casey or with him, should he decide to go.

LA: (inaudible)

IN: I understand you have a young daughter.

LA: Yes.

IN: And what is her name?

LA: Ruby.

IN: Are you here because you think your participation will in some way help protect her?

LA: Casey is hardly the key to my daughter's safety.

IN: If I were to tell you that my employers could ensure Ruby's safety from here on out, would that change your mind about staying here with Casey?

LA: No one can make that promise. Anyone who does is a liar.

IN: I have two children of my own—

LA: I don't mean to be rude, but I'm not sure why the fuck I should care.

IN: Well, I'm a therapist, but I am a mother first. And I can tell you I'd do just about anything to protect my children.

LA: Good for you.

IN: If you knew for certain you and Ruby would never have to worry about her father again, are you still here tomorrow?

LA: This is dumb. I'm not interested in hypotheticals.

IN: Do you love Casey?

LA: This is a question "the team" gave you?

IN: Our interest in your relationship with Casey is pertinent to our study of his abilities, yes.

LA: (inaudible)

IN: I'm sorry, what was that?

LA: He's a good person.

IN: Casey is a good person?

LA: A very good person.

IN: And you? Are you a good person, Lylian?

LA: I want to be.

IN: How long have you been with Casey?

LA: Not long. Under a year.

IN: When you first met him, what was the attraction?

LA: The Casey you met this morning isn't exactly the Casey I asked out eight or nine months ago, Doctor.

IN: I didn't mean to imply anything negative about his physicality, Lylian. Was it the way he looked then?

LA: Maybe. I don't know, I was just drawn to him.

IN: Was there something about him that made you believe he might be helpful in navigating your situation with Ruby?

LA: Hardly. I know I just said that he wasn't the version of Casey you met today, but it's not like he was some goddamn superhero.

IN: Okay then, gun to your head, what drew you to him?

LA: When was the last time you were single? The world isn't kind. Men aren't kind. Women aren't kind. Kindness is like fucking gold out there right now.

IN: He was kind to you, then.

LA: He was kind, and...

IN: Take your time.

LA: He was kind, then he became powerful. Or at least it seemed like he'd been given a gift that would make him powerful. A gift that might make *us* powerful.

IN: A man who claims he can foresee the future would make a powerful ally. I guess I can't deny that.

LA: You don't believe he can read, do you?

IN: It's a lot to digest.

LA: Is that a stab at humor?

IN: Ah, I see what I did there. Purely accidental, I assure you.

LA: How in the hell do you plan on helping Casey if you don't *believe* Casey?

IN: How far into your relationship was it when *you* decided to believe his visions were accurate?

LA: He read for one of my co-workers, a couple of weeks after his first premonition. She was an easy mark, no offense to Celia, but she was always talking about hippy-dippy shit during our shifts together. When I told her my new boyfriend was a psychic, I didn't have to twist her arm to get her to join us for cocktails at his place.

IN: And so, Celia came over to hang out with the two of you, knowing that Casey planned on reading for her?

LA: I don't think I was explicit on that when I invited her, no. But she was way into it when Casey suggested she let him read for her over dinner.

IN: Was it a large meal?

LA: Don't listen to Casey. Back then, normal-sized meals were plenty. Casey might tell you he's always needed to gorge, and he certainly believes it's necessary to see now, but in the early days, an average person would classify what he ate as nothing other than filling.

IN: And what he foresaw came to pass?

LA: It did.

IN: What was it that he predicted, or… what happened that he had seen? I'm sorry, I don't think I have the lingo down yet. It is hard to talk about this subject without sounding incredibly dim.

LA: Don't overthink it. In the vision, he found Celia sobbing uncontrollably in the storage room. She was texting back and forth with someone like her life depended on it. And this was all happening while some obscure folk song was playing through the café's ceiling speakers.

IN: What was happening?

LA: It wasn't nearly as horrible as it looked. A couple of days after the reading, while I was working, I found Celia there. Sure enough, she was hysterical. And she was texting like a crazy person. It took her a full minute or more to realize I was there. It turns out, it was just her boyfriend, he was breaking up with her. Well, breaking up with her while telling her that he had been fucking her mom. What he saw was true, though not tragic, relatively speaking.

IN: And the song?

LA: I don't know the track by name, but it was folk or folk-pop. It's not really my thing. Look, that one reading didn't clinch it for me entirely, but it didn't take many more tests for me to believe him.

IN: Isn't it just as likely that when he told Celia what he had seen of her future that she decided to act it out? Or at a minimum, play some role in bringing that exact scene to life... maybe unwittingly?

LA: C'mon, [redacted]. He didn't tell Celia what he'd *actually* seen. What the fuck kind of proof would that have been?

IN: Ah, of course.

LA: He made up some garbage about her being on a boat, off the coast of San Diego, I think he said. Only he and I knew what he had actually seen while visiting her timeline. She wasn't in on it, and I wasn't born yesterday.

IN: I didn't mean to suggest you were. That being said, people claiming to be psychics is nothing new. They're everywhere. Cities, strip malls, the boonies. Just search "psychics near me" and you're guaranteed to find a half-dozen willing to take your money.

LA: I'm not here to try and convince you that Casey's ability is legit, or convince anyone else for that matter.

IN: Surely you can understand how absurd this all sounds.

LA: If you don't want to believe it, take it up with Casey. You might want to run your disbelief by your employers. I don't know who the fuck they are, but it seems to me, they are definitely interested in what he is able to do. I can't imagine why they'd keep you on staff if you think he's bullshitting.

IN: A valid point.

LA: I didn't mean to lose my shit. It's wild, I know. And none of this is what I was hoping for when Casey and I sat down to that first dinner. But we let the genie out, and maybe I should have stuffed that motherfucker back into the bottle. I could have blown Casey off, I could have pretended not to be intrigued, I could have done a lot of things early on that would have put us on an entirely different timeline. Something far more normal.

IN: And what would that have looked like?

LA: I don't know. My life has never been what someone would refer to as normal. I'm not sure why I ever thought I might be able to work Ruby and me into something ordinary. I don't know much about ordinary living to begin with.

IN: I'm told you and Casey were charging people for his services as a psychic. Was that a mutual decision?

LA: It was his idea, but I didn't protest.

IN: But were you agreeable to the scheme?

LA: You are thinking that maybe I was just using him.

IN: In my role, I try to make absolutely no judgements.

LA: It's okay. If I were in your shoes, I'd probably think that.

IN: You were undecided on the idea of charging people, then? Or uncertain of how you felt about him reading at all?

LA: I was okay with it, at first. I was okay with a lot of what Casey had decided to do.

IN: And why was that?

LA: It's pretty fucking amazing when someone—someone you barely know—decides to put themselves through hell to make sure your life can become a fairy tale. Do you know what I mean?

IN: I'm afraid I can only imagine.

LA: That's a real shame, Doc. That kind of attention...

IN: Is addictive?

LA: I'm not sure there is a word to describe it.

IN: Why do you think he made that kind of commitment to you?

LA: He would have made the same commitment to someone else.

IN: You think?

LA: I'm not special. I was just the first woman to give him that opportunity.

IN: Were you thinking that maybe, at some point, Casey might stop?

LA: I asked him to stop reading a long time before things got out of hand. But I could have done more.

IN: It's not on you to change his behavior.

LA: I have had plenty of experience with recovery babble, please spare me the "my role" bullshit.

IN: It's obvious to me that you feel you bear some responsibility for where Casey finds himself now, but—

LA: Fuckin-A, Lady. I am the *only* reason Casey is where he finds himself now.

11

He is a needle.

But Casey is not hard to find. He is running among the beige of the desert around David's home. He wears a neon green shirt and matching shorts over his more common physique. There is also a black bracelet around his ankle. Its snug bind keeps the tracking device steady, right above the commotion of his bright red running shoe.

He races to one end of the property, then sets out toward the other. The drone above reverses direction just as quickly. Casey never outruns it, but he is giving it his very best shot.

The competition is interrupted. He stops in his tracks with the quickness of someone who has been bit. From his shoulder strap, he pulls out a smartphone. It vibrates in his hand, he looks to the screen. It reads, LYLIAN CELL. He runs a thin, sweaty finger over the screen to unlock it, wipes repeatedly until the action takes. Lylian's face fills the rectangle, traces of blue skies at its edges. The faint sound of the ocean accompanies her greeting.

"You're running, we can try you later."

She sounds like she is looking for any reason to kick their call further down the road.

"No, no, no, Lylian. I've got all day to run. Now is perfect." He finds respiratory balance. "It's been too long. And today is special."

Lylian's face contorts itself into agreement. "Okay, then. It's good to see you, Casey."

The drone hangs over their reunion. Casey takes a moment away from the screen to give the middle finger to its operator. The machine bends down as if to mock him, then whirrs its way home. He returns his attention to Lylian and she shoots for a bit of levity.

"I like your shirt, it's intense."

"Oh, thank you," he says. He holds the camera at an angle that showcases his full ensemble. "I have ten other outfits just like it. Easy to see, I guess." He brings the screen back down to his face to find his attempt at humor didn't land.

"You look good, Casey. You look…" she pauses. It's as if her brain is searching from a short list of adjectives that she knows are all wrong. "You look healthy," she finally manages.

"You mean heavy, but that's okay."

She doesn't try to persuade him otherwise. What would be the point?

"How is it where you are? Wherever you are?" he asks.

"We're good, Casey. We are… good."

Casey smiles.

"But, then again, maybe you already knew that," she adds.

For a moment, she brightens, sounds eager to hear that maybe his visions had shown him they would be doing well.

"I only read when David wants me to read, and for who David wants me to read for," Casey plainly admits. "I can't check out a timeline outside of those he assigns. I have no access to the kitchen here. I eat what the staff feeds me, and only when the staff is authorized to feed me."

What little light Lylian held in her eyes goes out.

"It's okay, Lylian. I chose this, remember?"

"He can't hold you there forever, Casey."

"He won't."

"I thought you said you weren't reading for yourself?"

"I'm not. Not anymore."

"So?"

"Look, let's not ruin today with speculations. Where is the birthday girl? Where is Ruby?"

Lylian sweeps her camera across a sun-soaked patio and holds it steady. Ruby is below deck, past it, on a pristine white sand beach, stomping around a sandcastle with a gaggle of little boys and girls.

"Mi cielito!" Lylian shouts. "Come up here and say hello to your Tío Casey."

Ruby stops in her tracks, then turns to protest.

"Not now, Mama! I'm playing—"

"Ahora, Ruby!" Lylian firmly demands.

"Don't worry about it, Lyl. Seriously, this is *her* day. Just give Ruby a giant hug for me and tell her I said happy birthday, okay?"

Lylian returns to the screen. Her cheeks are lightly flushed.

"I'm told seven is easier than six, so far I don't see it." She shakes her head, playfully admonishing the strengthening will of her child. "She's like you," Lylian half-jests. "Does what she wants."

"She's like her father," Casey says.

"Is there still a difference?" Lylian asks.

He shuts his eyes and regretfully exhales. The talk teeters on his more accurate comparison. They face each other through their screens, but neither can put their eyes on the other. For a while, the only sounds are of Ruby laughing with her friends as they tromp around the beach.

"Will you be around later?" she asks.

"We're having a big dinner tonight, actually. Well, I will be having a big dinner tonight, anyway."

"You are reading?"

"Mm-hmm," Casey manages.

"Should we try you before then?" Lylian asks.

"I'd like that, Lylian."

"Okay then, I'll have Ruby call you later," she says. "Take care of yourself, okay?"

"I've got plenty of people looking out for me, Lylian. You take care of Ruby, okay? I'll talk to you later."

"You will, I promise you will."

"I know. Bye, Lyl."

"Okay, then," she yields. "Bye."

His phone is tucked halfway behind the plastic shield of his running band, when he stops short of pushing the rest of the device all the way in. He listens, searches the sky for the drone. It has yet to return. Casey bends to a knee with the pretend intent of re-lacing a shoe. He grabs for a nearby rock, no bigger than his hand, then starts to chip at the hard-packed crust of the desert floor. A shallow hole forms, just deep enough for the phone. He plucks it from its black neoprene holder and gently places it into the ground. While looking over his shoulder, he buries the device in a hurry, hiding it under dirt and pebbles.

Casey stands, then stomps a foot on the loose fill. The tiny bump flattens, spreads, and blends into the landscape. He stares at the compound. Despite the distance, the smells of a gigantic meal in the making come and go on the breeze. When he returns his attention to himself, there is no indication of regret and he makes no attempt to retrieve the device from its tiny grave.

He loads up on a deep breath and sprints for the house. Despite running into a stiff wind, his eyes are absent of humanity. He is pushing his speed, incrementally lengthening the distance between heel strikes with each passing stride, as if he hopes to burst his own heart from the exertion alone.

The drone pops from its launch pad behind the stone walls of the rear courtyard. By the time its operator realizes where Casey is, the machine has overshot his location by a hundred yards. It lets out a shrill whirl as it changes course to catch up with its target. Its buzz is angry. It accelerates with impressive momentum, trying to reach him, but by the time it finds Casey, he has already crossed through the gate and into the courtyard. At best, it was a tie, a true photo finish, and the result is enough to return a small smile to Casey's face.

"How's Lylian?" David asks.

Casey finds David sitting in a lounge chair next to a very attentive drone operator. His short-lived victory over the drone crumbles. He folds his arms across his chest to hide the empty phone band on his left bicep.

"It was a good call, thanks," he says. "Not surprisingly, she didn't ask me to say hello to you."

The insult doesn't land, but David's face goes sideways as he tilts his head back. "Fuck, it's Ruby's birthday, isn't it?" Before Casey can confirm, David adds, "I'll ring her tonight."

"I'm sure you will."

The sounds coming from the kitchen are many. Dicing, chopping, the hot sizzle of grease, and the variable rumble of kitchen staff speaking to each other in Spanish. The subtle savor of mesquite wood and collection of meats grilling has an invisible stranglehold on the courtyard. David breathes it all in with huge exaggeration.

"I'm looking forward to your reading meal tonight, aren't you?"

Casey doesn't give an inch. "It all smells divine." He gauges David's mood and continues. "I was actually thinking I might get a head start on eating, if that's okay with you."

The suggestion excites David more than it should.

"That's the spirit, Big Brother! An appetizer. By all means, you eat however eating works best for you."

His attention quickly turns to the drone his man has landed at their feet. David picks up the drone and turns it over.

"Tell me again how this damn thing works," he says to the operator. "I mean *how* it flies, I know how to fly it."

Casey turns to leave. As he walks away from the burgeoning lesson on the physics of four rotors, David asks, "Hey, you didn't actually give Lylian all of your money, did you, Casey?"

"Dad's money, you mean?"

"Yes, that money."

"I'm certain you already know I did."

"I wonder…" David lets it hang. "What would Virginia Anne think about her son's charity if she were alive to see it, to see him in love."

Casey resumes his walk toward the kitchen.

"Fuck off, David."

"I can do that!" David bellows. "Until tonight, Casey. I'll see you tonight!"

Casey enters the compound's cookhouse unannounced. Here is the din at its source, loud and proud. For a moment, he remains unseen. The cooks and crew are so busy with their preparations they are oblivious to Casey's arrival. He relishes this moment of temporary invisibility. The commotion of a dozen skilled hands working knives on carrots, onions, potatoes, and more is hypnotic. Large pots of stew boil like witches' cauldrons, thick cuts of beef sizzle over flames, and on the perimeter of the half-outdoor galley, a row of blackened whole chickens spins slowly within an open-grill rotisserie.

A man in a tall white toque looks up, and seeing Casey brings an immediate recognition. He grins as he shuffles to one side of the kitchen, pointing to the rotisserie chickens the whole way there. When he squares himself in front of Casey, he can hardly contain his enthusiasm.

"Mister Casey, the special pollo you ask for, no?"

The cook's ask is in a broken, but practiced English. He hasn't stopped proudly pointing to the glistening bird bodies rotating to his left. Casey is excited the chef is so excited.

"Voy a empezar temprano, Jorge. Box one of those chickens for me, puedes?"

Jorge is already halfway to the chickens when he responds, "Sí, sí, Mister Casey. Uno momento!"

He gently removes a whole chicken from its spit forks, takes it to the counter to prepare it, then reaches for a big carving knife.

"As is, Jorge," Casey politely demands as he puts a hand to Jorge's arm. "Tomaré el pollo entero, I'll take it to go."

Puzzled, but with no authority over the matter, Jorge puts the blade aside. "As you wish, Mister Casey." His eyes go still as he searches his vocabulary. "Do you want for me to put chicken on a tray at least?"

"That would be perfect," Casey agrees. "Thank you."

While he waits, Casey helps himself to a bottled beverage from the kitchen's glass-door cooler. There is no hesitancy to his selection. He grabs a dark lager from the shelves, pinching the bottle's neck between his two fingers so he is able to grab the dolled-up chicken tray.

"Thanks, Jorge," he says gratefully. Jorge nods and the team sends Casey off with jubilant waves. Casey adds, "You guys be good now."

He carries the beer and the meal's platter to a grand indoor dining room adjacent to the rear courtyard. Through the room's oversized picture window, Casey can see David still clowning around with the drone outside. The black-box control screen is tight between his hands, and David is making haphazard adjustments to the drone's flight out over the desert. His crony nods along with a smile half encouraging and half anxious. Neither man is aware Casey is watching.

He situates himself at the table in a direction that allows him to keep tabs on David's preoccupation with the drone. The surface has already been set for dinner. It is not quite the elaborate set-up from the night that Cooper was killed. It has the look of something more routine. Nonetheless, it is awash in clean and unspoiled tableware. Using the edge of the tray in hand, he shoves a place setting into the others, then sets the chicken down upon the perfectly white linen. He sits on a long wooden bench in front of the bird, then twists the cap off the lager and brings it to his lips. With one eye on David, he guzzles the entirety of its liquid courage.

Starting with only the fingers on his hands, Casey begins to tear the meat away from the chicken's frame. The unpleasant undertaking comes with its own subtle soundtrack, squelching meat. He palpates all parts of the carcass, working his index finger over the cooked flesh and muscle left clinging to bone. Then he gnaws at what his fingers were unable to remove. Casey spits out the tiny bits of meat, depositing them all around the table and onto the floor. If possession were real, in this moment, Casey is a fine exhibit-A of what a demon could do.

When most of what was edible has been separated from the chicken's skeleton, Casey ends his rampage. If it weren't for all the bland shreds of sustenance discarded about the kill, one could easily assume that vultures had been responsible for picking the cooked bird clean.

Casey looks up from the mess. The kitchen sounds are just as loud as before. Out the window, David's focus is on whatever the drone's camera is broadcasting back to him. Casey leans from the waste, putting his face just above the exploited carcass. One by one, he investigates the exposed bones of the animal's skeleton, carefully surveying their varying contours by running his fingers from end to end on their shapes.

His right index finger finds an agreeable spike at the end of what may have been the chicken's clavicle or rib. He rests his fingertip upon it. Using his other hand, he searches for the pulsation of an artery beneath his jawline. For a split second, the tantalizing aromas wafting in from the cookhouse synthesize into one malodorous, overpowering tang. Casey looks out the window at David. He closes his eyes, then draws in all he can of the foul smell around him. It is one long and perfect inhalation.

How will the world know me.

The jabs he makes to his neck are many and quick. The pointed end of the bone punctures through the taught skin of his throat repeatedly. Each new rupture is deeper and more severe than the last. Casey's brutal assault on his jugular and carotid ends when he is truly unable to continue the attack. The last stab sticks. The bone juts out of his neck. A tiny off-white flag of surrender, waving amongst the rush of blood. Casey leaves it there as a disturbing euphoria slips over his face. With each dwindling beat of his heart, the perforations push his life outside of him.

Ambivalence is no longer present in his stare. As death approaches, his eyes burn more brightly. He fights to survive long enough to take in David's reaction as he and his men come running into the dining room. David's face is full of an incensed understanding. It is the look of a man who perfectly comprehends why he has been bested. In that moment, as Casey bleeds out, David has no one to blame but himself.

"Thank you, Little Brother," Casey manages before he can no longer balance his body.

He coughs, and the blood in the vaulting bark decorates the table and David's white pants in a victorious splatter. Casey sways to his right, and the sway gives way to an uncontrolled drop. His head crashes with a fantastic crack as it meets the unforgiving catch of the earthly-bronze ceramic tiles at everyone's feet. David quickly falls to a knee next to Casey—

—next to me.

Am I fucking dead? Jesus.

There, David finds me wearing a smug smile.

It's subtle, seems to shout, "I am free."

At least that's how I'd interpret the smile on my dead-as-fuck face.

The useless compressions David is making are violent and hard to see around.

Not surprising the little shit never bothered to learn CPR.

As it is, I've seen enough.

I'm coming out of the vision, I'm sure I could stay longer, but to what end?

Okay.

Well, that was fucked.

I mean, like for real fucked.

I can accept that David might be my brother, but no fucking way am I destined to off myself.

The Casey from that vision is not the Casey that I am.

Not the Casey that I can be.

It can't be.

I refuse to believe it.

I have no proof that any of us can change our futures.

I have no evidence to suggest that tiny deviations can affect my own timeline.

But, I'm not about to let what I've just seen—the version of me I've just watched—dictate our next move.

Tomorrow, Lylian and I run.

We'll go a different direction maybe.

We won't involve Lyl's mom.

Fuck it, we'll do everything different.

We will leave David's with the information I have and take our chances.

Then again...

Who the hell is Candace?

I've no fucking idea.

Why would I make that deal?

It doesn't matter. I don't care what I saw.
Is our fate our own to make?
I can't say for certain.
We leave tomorrow.
That is certain.
Now, if you'll excuse me, I've got to hit the toilet.

THE POWER YOU HOLD

Time is our most valuable commodity. I'd like to thank you for sharing some of yours with me. The deep gratitude I carry for every person who has ever taken the time to read something I've written has always been a difficult emotion to communicate. Thank you, thank you, thank you. Authors survive on word of mouth and reviews. A book's success is entirely up to a reader's willingness to shout about it. If you enjoyed *Future Skinny*, please tell a friend about it. And if you have just a few extra moments more, it'd mean the world to me if you could write a review on Amazon, Barnes & Noble, Goodreads, Google, or on any other site where you might have purchased this novel. If you didn't enjoy it, no worries. Please write a review for a book from another author. One that did move you. Believe me, even if it is years after you've read their story, the power you hold to immediately lift another human's whole being to the heavens, if only for a moment, is very real.

ALSO BY PETER ROSCH

My Dead Friend Sarah

But I Love You

Level 9 Paranoia

ABOUT THE AUTHOR

Peter Rosch is what happens when a Polish drag-racing varsity bowler and a beautiful, but über paranoid, French Canadian Air Force brat get together on a disco dance floor in glorious Albuquerque, NM. An award-winning writer whose decades in advertising, music, and film introduced him to more than a few bad habits. He hopes it wasn't for naught. Kirkus called his first novel, My Dead Friend Sarah, "a gripping story" in which "Rosch skillfully renders a unique story of a missing woman."